"Following me? You'd have done better to follow your master, Cabbarus, to the devil or wherever he is."

"I have to earn my living, sir."

"Spy? Informer? Worse, for all I know."

Skeit gave him a wounded look. "Those are very hard words, sir. I do my work. I have no grudge against you."

"No business with me, either."

"Now, there, sir, allow me to disagree." Skeit reached into his cloak. "You understand, it's not a matter of ill will. That's not my nature."

Skeit's pudgy hand, when it emerged, held a pistol. With the deftness of an expert at his trade, he cocked the weapon, took precise aim, and fired.

LLOYD ALEXANDER, a resident of Drexel Hill, Pennsylvania, is the author of *Westmark* and The Prydain Chronicles, including *The Book of Three, The High King, Taran Wanderer, The Black Cauldron,* and *The Castle of Llyr,* all available in Dell Laurel-Leaf editions.

"Following me! You'd have done better to follow your master, Cabbarus, to the devil or wherever he is."

"I have to earn my living, sir."

"Spy? Informer? Worse, for all I know."

Skeit gave him a wounded look. "Those are very hard words, sir. I do my work. I have no grudge against you."

"No business with me, either."

"Now, there, sir, allow me to disagree." Skeit reached into his cloak. "You understand, it's not a matter of ill-will. That's not my nature."

Skeit's pudgy hand, when it emerged, held a pistol. With the deftness of an expert at his trade, he cocked the weapon, took precise aim, and fired.

Lloyd Alexander, a resident of Drexel Hill, Pennsylvania, is the author of *Westmark* and The Prydain Chronicles, including *The Book of Three*, *The High King*, *Taran Wanderer*, *The Black Cauldron*, and *The Castle of Llyr*, all available in Dell Laurel-Leaf editions.

ALSO AVAILABLE IN LAUREL-LEAF BOOKS:

WESTMARK, *Lloyd Alexander*

THE BOOK OF THREE, *Lloyd Alexander*

THE BLACK CAULDRON, *Lloyd Alexander*

THE CASTLE OF LLYR, *Lloyd Alexander*

TARAN WANDERER, *Lloyd Alexander*

THE HIGH KING, *Lloyd Alexander*

THE BOY WHO SAVED EARTH, *Jim Slater*

A WRINKLE IN TIME, *Madeleine L'Engle*

A WIND IN THE DOOR, *Madeleine L'Engle*

A SWIFTLY TILTING PLANET, *Madeleine L'Engle*

# THE KESTREL

LLOYD ALEXANDER

LAUREL-LEAF BOOKS bring together under a single imprint outstanding works of fiction and nonfiction particularly suitable for young adult readers, both in and out of the classroom. Charles F. Reasoner, Professor Emeritus of Children's Literature and Reading, New York University, is consultant to this series.

Published by
Dell Publishing Co., Inc.
1 Dag Hammarskjold Plaza
New York, New York 10017



ISBN: 0-440-94393-0

RL: 6.9

Reprinted by arrangement with E. P. Dutton, Inc.
Printed in the United States of America
October 1983
10 9 8 7 6

WFH

For those who know that
they are only human but who
try not to be any less

# CONTENTS

# PART I

# THE BEGGAR QUEEN

WESTMARK
Dorning
DOMITIAN MOUNTAINS
Freyborg
Nierkeeping
Marianstat
Belvitsa
REGIA
Altus-Birkenfeld
Mull
Carlsbruch
THE FINGERS
Eschbach
DOMITIAN MOUNTAINS
Water Rats
N
W
E
S

# 1

Spring in the Carla River valley was a matter of opinion. The day had begun gently. By dusk, when Theo reached the little inn at Mull, it was spitting hard, grainy snow.

He made sure his horse was decently stabled, then carried what little baggage he had into the public room. Near the fire, a traveler sat carefully scraping his boots. With his windburned face and patch of gray hair, he could have been any kind of steady, reliable journeyman who did his own work and minded his own business.

Theo stopped short. The steady, reliable journeyman, when Theo last saw him, had been galloping like a maniac on a stolen cavalry mount, his shirt in bloody tatters.

Theo dropped his traveling case. "Luther?"

The man recognized him at the same instant and in a couple of long-legged strides came to greet him, looking him up and down with easy familiarity.

"The latest fashion in Marianstat?" Luther's glance took in the stained cloak and scuffed boots.

"I wouldn't know." Theo grinned back at him. "I haven't been there for—it must be six months now."

"Alone? The future prince of Westmark without a dozen lackeys following?"

"I did have one," said Theo. "He worked very hard at stealing my clothes and selling them. Apart from that, he did nothing; so I finally sent him back to court."

"The right place for a lazy rascal. Now, lad, what brings you to Mull?"

"I'm on my way to the Carla Col. I want to see the mountains, and the Horngard. And you? I don't think you're here to admire the scenery."

"No."

"What then?"

"Business."

Theo knew better than to press for explanations. Instead, he asked, "How is Florian?"

"As always. Himself."

Theo nodded. They had been there, all of them, the day Florian raided the Nierkeeping arsenal: Mickle—he could never think of her now as Princess Augusta; Count Las Bombas and Musket. And Zara, the russet divinity; Stock, the poet, roaring at the top of his voice. Florian's companions, those he called "my children," who would have followed him anywhere—as Theo might have done. He remembered himself that morning, pistol raised; and another of Florian's children, half his face slashed open.

He hesitated, then asked, "What about Justin?"

"With Florian. He's well. Remarkably well."

The room was filling with travelers driven in by the snow. Luther motioned with his head. "Talk in my room."

Theo shouldered his bag and followed, stopping at the foot of the stairs to ask the landlord if any packet had come for him from Marianstat. The landlord, with a kitchen cloth tied around his neck, was entertaining his cronies in an alcove behind the serving counter, trying to play a hand of cards and wait on his guests at the same time. He ducked into the alcove and came back to advise there was none.

Luther had overheard Theo's inquiry. "Do you get much news from the palace?"

"Not as much as I'd like. Mickle—Princess Augusta—writes to me. So does Chief Minister Torrens. They're never sure where I'll be, and neither am I. By the time anything catches up with me it could be weeks. I send them word whenever I find a dispatch rider. It gets there sooner or later."

"Money?"

"Enough. I have a treasury warrant. King Augustine himself signed it. Do you need anything?"

Luther winked. "You can buy supper for us later."

Luther unbolted a door at the head of the stairs. The chamber was small, and the slope of the raftered ceiling made it appear still more cramped. Except for a pair of saddlebags in the corner, there was no sign it had been much lived in. The table was bare, the straw mattress unrumpled. The fire had nearly burned out in the hearth.

"The landlord claims it's the best room in the house." Luther lit a candle stub. He squatted at the fireplace and blew on the embers. "I hope he's lying. Now, let's hear about your grand tour."

"Not very grand," said Theo, "but it suits me better this way. I can see more on my own." He gave Luther a wry smile. "Sometimes I wonder if Augustine wants me to learn about the kingdom or if he just wants me anywhere but at the Juliana Palace. No—that's not fair. He means well. I could have stayed. It was my choice.

"Even so," he went on, "I still wonder. Mickle doesn't care a rap if she's a princess and I'm a commoner. For Queen Caroline, it's bad enough that I was a printer's devil. Worse, that I had anything to do with Florian. The courtiers already make it a royal scandal."

"Meanwhile, they pack you off sightseeing."

"I've done more than that." From his jacket, he took a wad of papers, closely written, tied about with string. "I've been keeping a journal. What I've seen, what I've done. I've talked with bailiffs, stewards, tenant farmers. I've been looking at town archives, too; estate accounts when I can get at them. I put down all the figures: how much yield for an artistocrat's land, how much more for a freeholder's. There's no question, it strikes you in the face—"

"That the aristocracy's made a botch of it," put in Luther. "Embarrassing discovery for a future prince."

"I copied the figures and sent them to Torrens and the king. They can see for themselves."

Luther chuckled. "You're a born troublemaker. You should have stayed with us."

"No. There must be another way to set things right. Not trying to pull down the monarchy. There's terrible poverty in the countryside; in the towns, too, for that matter. But if it could be worked out fairly, everyone would be better off. It's common sense—"

"It's common sense to end the monarchy altogether. Start with that, not with how many bushels of corn to an acre."

"That's only your way of looking at it."

"Mine. And a great many others'."

Theo put back his papers. Argument was useless. Luther, like Florian, had set on one path and would see no other. What troubled Theo was whether they understood things more clearly than he did. He brightened as he reached into the traveling case. "I've been doing something else."

He brought out his sketchbook and opened it on the table. Since leaving Marianstat, he had taken the habit of drawing. At first, it merely passed the time. But lately it had become more than idle amusement. If a day passed without adding to his sketches, he felt unsatisfied and empty.

Luther paged through the book, now and then stopping to look closer at a scene: a peasant woman and her child; a gaggle of street urchins; a fishwife; a carpenter planing a board. "That's Westmark. Not your accounts and archives."

Theo warmed his hands at the fire. Something had come into his mind the moment he had seen Luther in the public room. The older man appeared content to go on studying the drawings.

Theo finally turned. "You knew I'd be here. You were waiting."

"Yes." Luther glanced up. "Florian wanted to send greetings."

"What else? Come straight out."

"General Erzcour. He commands the Carla military region."

"I know. He's a good officer, I've heard. What of him?"

"Florian says Erzcour must be replaced. If you press

your chief minister to do it, he'll pay attention. He'll listen to one of his own people."

"I'm not one of his own people. Or anybody's."

Luther raised his hands in mock defense. "Don't get ruffled. I didn't mean it that way."

"However you meant it, Erzcour's none of my business. I can't guess what Florian has in mind. Perhaps I don't want to. He's my friend, but I don't agree with him. He knows that. How can he ask me this kind of favor?"

"He sees it the other way round."

"Florian doing the monarchy a favor? Why?"

Luther shrugged. "Does it matter?" He closed the book. "Take it as a favor or whatever. Only make sure Erzcour's dismissed. Pensioned off. Anything. So long as he has no troops under him.

"The king wants to make reforms. I'll give him that much credit," Luther went on. "But some of the aristocracy and the military won't stomach them. We don't know how many are in the faction, but they're up to some kind of mischief. It's a good guess Erzcour's with them."

"You have proof?" Theo tried to stay calm. Even before he left Marianstat, there had been rumors of conspiracies, cabals, plots by disgruntled courtiers. They had, fortunately, turned out to be overblown gossip. "There's evidence against him?"

"Not yet. Florian suspects—"

"Only suspects?" broke in Theo. "Luther, the king will want more than that. The law demands proof beyond question. When Cabbarus was chief minister, honest folk were ruined, even hanged, on nothing but suspicion. Augustine won't let that kind of thing happen again. Neither will any of us."

"Very admirable," returned Luther. "Do you think Erzcour and his friends will stick at fine points of law? Don't be a fool. Florian's given you a warning. Take it or not."

Theo did not answer. Something was stirring below in the public room. He heard voices raised, but not in argument or rough joking. The tone was agitated yet subdued, an unsettling sound. Luther, too, noticed and stepped to the door, listening. He motioned Theo to stay behind and strode quickly downstairs. Theo waited a few moments, then, as the commotion went on, started after him.

Luther, returning, met Theo at the head of the stairs and drew him back into the room. "A wool dealer just up from Carlsbruch. He heard it two days ago. Augustine is dead. He died last week."

Theo caught his breath. In her last letter, Mickle had mentioned only briefly that her father was ailing. That had been midwinter. If she had sent a later message, it had not reached him. He stared at Luther. Telling himself the day would come sooner or later, he had never quite believed it. "Then—Mickle's queen of Westmark."

"Long live the queen," said Luther, not unkindly, though his words had an ironic edge to them. "And the prince consort. Like it or not, you're a monarchist as much as anyone can be."

"What you said about Erzcour and the rest—do you think they had a hand in this?"

"I don't know. Kings die from time to time."

"I'm going to Marianstat." Theo started buckling his traveling case. "The landlord can let me have a fresh horse."

"Stay the night," said Luther. "No sense being on the road at this hour. Your courtiers can wait."

"The courtiers can go hang. It's Mickle I care about. I should be with her. She'll wonder why I'm not there already. I'll save a day if I leave now. Tell Florian I'll get to the bottom of this Erzcour business. If it's true, he's done Mickle a service and I thank him."

"It won't rub my conscience too raw, associating with royalty," said Luther. "I'll ride a little way with you."

"I'll go faster alone."

"Likely so. Farewell, then." He took Theo's arm. "What's the matter? You don't have the look of a gallant off to join his sweetheart, let alone a prince consort to join his queen."

"It's—nothing." He turned away, picking up his bag. "It took me by surprise."

For a young man with every prospect of happiness, he did not want to admit how alarmed he was.

Half an hour out of Mull, the horse cast a shoe. Theo reined up at the side of the road and dismounted, berating the landlord who had sworn the animal was fit, and himself for not making sure of it in spite of his haste. He pulled up his collar and muffled his face for a cold tramp back to the inn.

The snow, at least, had stopped. The moon had risen bright and sharp-edged. Far below, at the foot of the rocky embankment, the Carla River glinted with a film of ice. Leading his limping mount, Theo bent his head against the wind.

He stopped at the sound of hoofbeats. Another horseman was coming at a brisk pace from the direction of the town. He glimpsed a squat figure crouched in the saddle. Sighting Theo, the rider halted and called out.

Surprised to hear his name, but glad for any help that might be forthcoming, Theo ran toward him. The rider, meantime, had swung nimbly to the ground. Short and dumpy, wrapped in a trailing cloak, he raised a finger to the brim of his hat.

"I knew it would be you, sir. But no harm in making certain, is there?"

The voice was not one Theo could forget. The little man's face was shadowed now, but clear enough in Theo's memory: the plump cheeks, the moist, pink-rimmed eyes. The name sprang to his lips without his having to think of it.

"Skeit."

The man bobbed his head. "You remember, sir? In the ordinary way of things, I'd prefer it otherwise. In your case, I take it as a compliment.

"I lost track of you for a time, sir, and nearly missed you again at Mull," he went on cheerfully. "When the landlord told me a young gentleman of your description went galloping off for Marianstat, I knew I'd come on the right path again."

"Following me? You'd have done better to follow your master, Cabbarus, to the devil or wherever he is."

"I have to earn my living, sir."

"Spy? Informer? Worse, for all I know."

Skeit gave him a wounded look. "Those are very hard words, sir. I do my work. I have no grudge against you."

"No business with me, either."

"Now, there, sir, allow me to disagree." Skeit reached into his cloak. "You understand, it's not a matter of ill will. That's not in my nature."

Skeit's pudgy hand, when it emerged, held a pistol. With the deftness of an expert at his trade, he cocked the weapon, took precise aim, and fired.

# 2

Queen Mickle urgently needed a few handfuls of dirt. She had not, until tonight, realized how scarce it was. Her apartments had, as always, been swept and dusted relentlessly.

Her need had sprung up suddenly at the end of the day. That morning, when Dr. Torrens, her chief minister, arrived still without word of Theo, Mickle's patience, even then, was scraped to the bone.

"All I want," she said, in a tone as reasonable as she could manage, "is a simple answer to a simple question: Where is he?"

Torrens shook his head. "We have no further news, Majesty, beyond what we already know."

"Which is nothing." Mickle paced the private audience chamber, hands clenched in the pockets of the breeches she wore in preference to the cumbersome skirts she suffered at grand ceremonials.

"The wheels of government turn slowly," said Torrens.

"Oiled with molasses," Mickle snapped. Dispatches

from local constables throughout the Carla valley, where Theo's last letter had come from, were no help. Her hopes had risen at the report of an innkeeper in a town called Mull. He dimly remembered selling a horse to a young man resembling Theo, but had no idea what had become of either. The clue led only to a blind alley. The officers Mickle sent from Marianstat had learned no more.

"Have you heard from Erzcour?" she demanded.

"The general advises he is eager to serve in any way he can. He offers troops to search the valley as soon as Your Majesty gives him specific information."

"In other words," replied Mickle, "I tell him where Theo is and he'll go find him."

Dr. Torrens watched her with concern. The girl, slight of frame, narrow waisted, with jutting shoulders, looked more street sparrow than imperial eagle. Unlike her mother, the new queen was no beauty at first glance. Yet there were times when her pale blue eyes made the air crackle, for she could show the bearing and presence of a sovereign—when she chose—and her quick mind absorbed all it lighted on. She might even become, he speculated, the strongest of the royal line. But she still had much to learn, Torrens thought sadly, and one hard lesson was now before her.

"I urge you, Majesty, to put aside your personal cares. All that can be done is being done. A ruler does not neglect affairs of state for affairs of the heart. The monarchy continues, while the heart—"

"What are you telling me?" cried Mickle. "That I'm supposed to go on, business as usual, and Theo missing for—"

"That is exactly what I am telling you," Torrens broke in bluntly. "When your father believed you dead, he lost himself in grief—and nearly lost the kingdom to Cabbarus. Your private concerns are your own, and must remain so, for you are a queen first and foremost." His tone softened. "Your work will make your waiting easier."

As Mickle did not answer, the white-haired chief minister laid a stack of documents on her desk. "To begin, the question of Baron Montmollin's landholdings must be dealt with."

"I don't see any question," Mickle said. "His family took common land that everyone was allowed to use for grazing or farming and made it part of their private estate. Theo wrote to us about it. He found proof when he was digging through some sort of town archives. The records show it was barefaced thievery."

"Undeniably common land," said Torrens, "but it was added to the principal estate, La Jolie, two generations ago."

"Thievery doesn't count if it's big enough and old enough? Montmollin already has more acres than anyone can keep track of. Add them up, he likely owns half of Westmark. Well, this much he'll have to give back to his tenants, no matter which of his noble ancestors stole it."

"Beyond a doubt, this should be done," said Torrens. "But not hastily. It is not the moment. I urge you to act with greatest deliberation."

"Delay, you mean," said Mickle. "If it's an old grievance, the more reason to set it right as soon as possible."

"I do not advise it," replied Torrens. "The whole aristocracy will feel threatened and turn against you. Landless and landed alike throughout the kingdom will demand investigation of all such holdings; some rightfully, others merely seizing a chance for gain. It can lead only to disorder. Since your father's death, the monarchy is in too delicate a balance. Make no move to disturb it. When your position is stronger, you may do so. Until then, follow a policy of discretion."

"And don't step on any toes," Mickle retorted. "You, of all people, advise that? You risked your life standing up to Cabbarus. You weren't exactly discreet then. Now you sound like a courtier."

Torrens stiffened. Color rose to his face. "I am no courtier, Majesty, nor will I ever be. I offer you my best judgment, for the good of the kingdom—and yours. If you believe otherwise, I ask you to choose another chief minister."

"Oh, Torrens, you know that's not what I meant," cried Mickle, going to him. The former Royal Physician was her strongest resource: an honest, forthright man whom she had now unwittingly hurt. The moment passed; Torrens regained his composure, but withdrew soon after, leaving the Montmollin affair unsettled.

Later, with her mother, Mickle was on the fine edge of tears for the first time since Theo's disappearance. "I don't understand it," she burst out. "I don't know why they can't find him."

Queen Caroline stroked her daughter's hair. "There is a possibility you must consider. A harsh one."

"That he's had an accident? Or could even be dead?"

said Mickle. "That's a possibility I won't consider at all."

"No," said Caroline. "Perhaps he cannot be found because he does not wish to be found."

Mickle frowned, puzzled, as the queen went on. "Six months is long in a young life. Love sworn one day is forgotten the next. This may be the case with your Theo. You, my child, must not allow it to break your heart. Affections change quickly. He would not be the first young man to find another sweetheart."

"I won't think that of him," Mickle snapped. "I don't see how you can think it, either."

She did not believe a word of what Queen Caroline had said.

She wondered if it might be true.

The rest of the day had been no happier than the beginning. She finally closeted herself in her apartments. Having given orders to admit no one, she was all the more vexed when a lady-in-waiting informed her of an individual claiming to be a nobleman who sought an audience; who, in fact, insisted on it.

Before Mickle could give a tart answer, a paunchy figure in a uniform glittering with medals thrust aside the indignant courtier. To the further shock of the lady-in-waiting, Mickle sprang up the instant she laid eyes on the intruder and threw her arms around as much of him as she could compass. A ginger-haired dwarf, with an enormous cocked hat under his arm, had also stumped into the room.

"Count Las Bombas!" she cried. "Musket! I thought you'd gone off to make your fortune!"

"My dear girl—dear Queen, that is," answered the portly count, "the less said about that the better." Despite the splendor of his uniform, he presented less than his customary cheerfulness; his moustache hung wilted, his cheeks sagged. "We're back from our travels and heard the news only a few days ago. I came as fast as I could to pay my respects. Which, alas, is all I'm in a position to pay."

"As usual, down to the last penny," grumbled Musket, "and he borrowed that one from me. I don't expect to see it again."

"Nonsense," protested Las Bombas. "I find myself in merely, what shall I call it, a fiscal pause."

"What about your elixir?" Mickle asked. "Your rejuvenating potions?"

"Excellent as ever," the count replied. "I wish I could say likewise for the customers."

"If things get worse," said Musket, "he might have to make an honest living."

"A prospect I intend to avoid at all cost," said the count. "I have already attempted to tread the path of rectitude and can attest that virtue is its own reward; indeed, its only reward. Marvelously satisfying in a dreary sort of way. Along the lines of meat and drink, however, it leaves something to be desired. I prefer to admire it at a safe distance."

During this, knowing the count's inclinations, Mickle had ordered that food be immediately brought for her visitors. Las Bombas attacked his victuals the instant they arrived. If his fortunes had suffered, his appetite had survived undamaged. Musket, though half the size of his master, boasted an equal capacity.

"We've tried everything," Las Bombas went on between mouthfuls. "My finest attractions: hypnotism, fortune-telling, sleight of hand. They met with a remarkably strong lack of interest. Ah, my dear, I long for those golden days—golden in every sense of the word—when we were all together. What a superb Oracle Priestess you were! And Theo—if he'd stayed with me he could have blossomed into a first-class mountebank, he had a gift for it. Where is he, by the way? Occupied, no doubt, with his princely duties? He's one to take that kind of work seriously: a flaw in an otherwise promising character; but he can't help it. Send for him, my dear. I'm eager to see the lad."

"So am I," said Mickle. "He's vanished. Not a word, not a trace." She quickly told Las Bombas what had happened and how all efforts to find him had failed.

"Impossible. People don't vanish into thin air. In the days of Cabbarus, yes. Not anymore. He must be somewhere."

"I know that," said Mickle. "Tell it to those bumblers searching for him. There's been so much delay, shilly-shallying, dispatches sent back and forth, it makes my teeth ache.

"Will you do me a service?" she continued, following an idea that had been in her mind since Las Bombas arrived. "The payment will be very worth your while."

"Accept money from a friend? Never!" declared Las Bombas. "Yes, well," he added hastily, "it's better than accepting it from a stranger. My dear Mickle, I should be delighted to oblige you without thought of compensation. Since you've thought of it, however, I'd not be so insensitive to refuse."

"Do you still have your coach? And Friska?"

"Both in fine state. The coach does not require nourishment, and Friska is content with her modest portion of hay. I wish I could say as much for myself. Yes, we all stand ready at your command."

"I want you to go to Mull, in the Carla valley, for a start," said Mickle. "Theo could have been there just before he disappeared. Wherever he is, find him. You and Musket can do it better and faster than all the troops, constables, and inspectors put together. You'll have money, as much as you want. I'll order the Royal Treasurer to give it to you now, cash in hand."

"Excellent!" Las Bombas heaved himself to his feet. "We'll turn him up for you. Consider it done. We depart immediately."

"No," said Mickle. "Not until tonight. There are too many busybodies in the palace during the day, too many noses in other people's affairs."

"I don't see what difference it makes."

"Because," Mickle said, "I'm going with you."

The count stared at her. "The queen of Westmark? Personally? Out of the question! It's—it's not fitting. It's beneath royal dignity."

"Blast royal dignity," said Mickle. "Besides, I won't let on I'm queen of anything. I'd never get the truth out of anybody. You'll think of something we can pretend to be. Torrens can manage without me for a while. I'll leave a note for my mother where she'll be sure not to find it until it's too late to send after me."

"My dear girl, it simply won't do. The hardships of the journey—"

"We've gone through worse," Mickle said. "I'm afraid something's happened to him. My mother has the notion he's changed his mind, that he doesn't want us to marry. That—that he's set his heart on somebody else. I don't believe it, but if it's true I want him to tell me so. To my face, straight out."

"I'm sure it's not the case," the count said. "Even if it were— Great heavens, girl, you can't ask me to be responsible for your safety and comfort."

"I'll answer for my own safety and comfort. Of course, if you don't want to take me with you, I won't force you."

Las Bombas sighed with relief. "Now you're being sensible."

Mickle grinned at him. "I'll go alone." While the count sputtered a protest, she added, "Naturally, then, you couldn't expect to be paid."

"Where your safety is concerned, mere gold cannot influence me in the slightest. It's a matter of reasonable judgment, of conscience." The count puffed out his cheeks and passed a hand over his brow. "Ah—there's no question. You'd be better off with us. Very well, I agree. It's my patriotic duty."

Las Bombas having yielded to conscience and duty, Mickle instructed him to make everything ready for their departure. To speed him on his way and protect him from a sudden attack of afterthoughts, she wrote out a treasury draft which she put into the reliable hands of Musket, telling the dwarf to have the coach waiting that night in an alley beyond the palace.

So it happened that Queen Mickle, as the Juliana bells rang midnight, urgently needed a supply of dirt.

Until half a year ago, Mickle had spent most of her life as a street urchin. She was able, thus, to slip into that role again with great ease and even greater enjoyment: It was a welcome relief.

Though she had also been an eager student of housebreaking, apprenticed to one of the finest burglars in Westmark, she understood that leaving the Juliana by stealth would present a few unique difficulties for the ruler. Guards of honor lined the corridors, sentries were posted throughout the courtyard and at the gates. The disguise of urchin would be essential in rejoining Las Bombas. The queen of Westmark, Mickle realized, had much power and little freedom.

She ripped and frayed a pair of breeches and a shirt until they looked properly disreputable. She could not say as much for herself. She had tied back her hair and scuffed her boots; but she needed grime, and the apartments were disgustingly clean. Mickle tried the fireplace. The day had been mild, no fire had been lit, and all traces of ash had been swept away. Reaching up the chimney, she finally scraped off an ample amount of soot, which she streaked over her face and hands and rubbed into her clothing.

Satisfied with her new appearance, Mickle opened the casement and stepped out onto the ledge. She swung nimbly upward and clambered to the rooftop, stopping just short of the peak. From there, flattened against the roof, she pressed along silent as a shadow in the direction of the palace wall until she reached a corner that would let her descend without having to cross too large an expanse of open courtyard.

A sentry paced below. Mickle slid easily down the nearest rainspout, stopping a short distance above the ground. She had planned to go the rest of the way as soon as the man's back was turned. He was infuriatingly slow. Instead of continuing his patrol, he stopped, leaned his musket against the side of the building, and yawned leisurely, giving every sign of lingering some while.

Silently berating him for a lazy lout, she decided to wait no longer. Las Bombas had ranked her among the best mimics and ventriloquists he had known. Relying on those gifts, Mickle took a deep breath.

An instant later, seemingly from around the corner nearest the sentry post, came a furious meowing and spitting, followed by barks, growls, and yelps. The guardsman seized his musket and ran to settle the most ferocious cat-and-dog fight he had ever heard.

Mickle grinned with satisfaction. She had lost none of her skill. She dropped to the flagstones and raced across the courtyard. Legs pumping, she struck the wall at full tilt. Her speed and momentum carried her halfway up. Her fingers caught at the slightest handholds in the cracks and crevices. Gaining the top, she swung over without breaking stride and dropped lightly to the street.

She crouched a moment in the darkness. Her mimicry had roused the kennels. From the palace grounds rose the baying of every hound in the royal pack, and the shouts of their bewildered keepers.

Mickle vanished into the shadows.

# 3

The ram was a magnificent specimen, with horns thick as a man's forearm curling above the shaggy brow. Deep-chested, coated with long white fleece, it lay on its side against an outcropping of rocks. It was not quite dead.

Three men in hunting costume, followed by their gun loaders and the local foresters, walked briskly over the stony ground. Afternoon sunlight sparkled on the blue white peaks of the Domitians, the high range at the eastern border of Westmark. The hunters were some leagues beyond this frontier, well within the neighboring kingdom of Regia.

"Bravo, General!" Duke Conrad of Regia clapped his hands. He was a stocky man with ruddy cheeks. "Excellent shot! They are elusive beasts, one rarely sees them. A favorable omen for your visit. I congratulate you."

"Your Highness promised good hunting." General Erzcour tended toward fleshiness. His large, heavy face and prominent cheekbones made his eyes appear especially bright and sharp. He had the habit of slightly pursing his lips, which made him look as if he were about to taste something pleasant. "We have not been disappointed."

"Certainly not in the matter of Regian game." The third huntsman, Baron Montmollin, was the tallest of the party. Although the eldest, he showed little trace of age in his finely drawn features. Hunting, for the most part, bored him; he strode along with his companions, an expression of polite indulgence on his face.

"Nor shall you be disappointed in anything else, I assure you," said Conrad. "We are largely in agreement already; the small matters can be settled quickly and happily."

They halted a few paces from the ram. It was watching them. The animal struggled to lift its head and make a thrust with its horns.

Duke Conrad turned to Erzcour. "The locals call these creatures rock rams. The more proper term is Domitian mouton. Is this your first? Splendid! You must indulge us, General, by observing one of our Regian customs."

He gestured to the chief forester. Drawing his hunting knife, the man walked up to the ram and cut its throat. Duke Conrad knelt and dipped his fingertips.

"Allow me, General. It is a very old custom. These mountain fellows would be much put out if it were not observed." He touched Erzcour's forehead and cheeks, leaving imprints like scarlet flowers.

"Now, Erzcour," said Baron Montmollin, "you look quite the savage."

"As a warrior should be," replied the duke. He wiped his fingers on a handkerchief and threw it aside. "I would even suggest," he went on jokingly, "that our troops follow the example of those native tribes that paint their faces to terrify their enemies."

"Some of our older court ladies," rejoined Montmollin, "have already adopted that practice."

Conrad, laughing at the baron's sally, ordered the foresters to deal with the carcass and led his guests down the slope. They were in high good humor by the time they reached a clearing in the wooded valley, where grooms waited with the horses.

There was no sign of King Constantine, who was to join them there. A groom reported that His Majesty had sighted a stag at the last moment and had set off after it.

"We shall not wait for him," Conrad told his visitors. "My nephew sometimes lets impulse, instead of policy, lead him. He knows where to find us. I can speak for him in his absence."

"I hope Your Highness can also speak for his safety," Erzcour said.

"Have no concern," replied the duke. "He is an excellent huntsman." He added lightly, "In any case, should some untoward event occur, the crown would revert to his eldest blood relative. And so, gentlemen, you would simply have me to deal with. That would not be disagreeable to you and your colleagues? Speaking theoretically, of course. Your plans would not be affected. We Regians, once fixed on a course of action, maintain it." He cocked an eye at the baron. "Your present sovereign is not so reliable. Unfortunate. I hear, Baron, she is called the Beggar Queen."

"So she is," replied Montmollin, "and I would prefer to see her queen of beggars instead of queen of Westmark. We are adequately provided with beggars on the streets; we do not require one on the throne."

The duke and his party rode back at an invigorating pace to the royal lodge. In the main room, where trophies of antlers and animal heads covered the walls, a table had been set with refreshments. Conrad motioned for the servants to withdraw. The baron had strolled to the gun racks and was examining a silver-mounted pistol.

"An exquisite weapon," observed Montmollin. "It would make death almost charming."

"Almost, but not quite." Conrad laughed. "Keep it, Baron. I see you are a connoisseur. As for death, I must say frankly that your king's demise has made our task easier. Your Beggar Queen is new to her throne. She has not, I gather, consolidated any great support among her ministers, the army, or even her subjects. It is our moment of opportunity. We must act quickly, however, before that moment is lost to us."

"We are prepared to do so," Montmollin said, going to the table. "The first move, my dear Duke, is up to you."

"Our course of action is simple," said Conrad. "General Erzcour has already communicated with my staff officers. They agree that Regian troops will attack Westmark through the Carla Col. After a token resistance, General Erzcour will surrender and order all units to do likewise. We shall advance through the Carla valley. The way will be clear for us to press on to Marianstat and capture it. We shall offer generous terms, insisting only on the abdication of the queen. She will be in no position to refuse.

"So, gentlemen, I see no difficulties," Conrad went

on. "For the sake of appearance, however, I believe it would be wise for you, General, to be taken prisoner temporarily, and treated with all the respect we pay to a gallant adversary. I also suggest that you, dear Baron, remain with us instead of returning to your estates. Not a hostage, you understand, but an honored guest. A small gesture of good faith. The king would appreciate this."

Montmollin bowed. "I accept your delightful hospitality. An unexpected pleasure, though I did not imagine my good faith required demonstration."

Erzcour had been listening with growing concern. "A soldier's oath is not taken lightly," he began after some hesitation. "Nor can it be broken lightly."

Conrad frowned. "Second thoughts? At this late stage?"

"General Erzcour is a good soldier," said Montmollin. "If he is suffering pangs of conscience, I quite understand and commend him." He turned to Erzcour. "You are not breaking your oath, I assure you. In the highest sense, you are keeping it. You are not betraying your kingdom. Nor am I. We are preserving it. The aristocracy is its blood and bone. Who can better hold it together? Yokels and cobblers? Tradesmen? The so-called educated classes are no better than rabble who have learned how to spell. The aristocracy alone stands above greed and self-interest. Your duty lies with us."

"I do not question my duty," said Erzcour. "What I require is clear agreement on my resistance at the Carla Col. My troops cannot lay down their arms without offering a genuine show of strength. Will Regia accept the necessary casualties?"

"Of course," replied Conrad. "The invasion must be convincing. But not exaggerated. In the first engagements, we would expect to sacrifice, say, one hundred men. And you? How many of your own before you would judge surrender as the correct military decision?"

"I estimate three hundred," said Erzcour. "To lose fewer would be for me to surrender dishonorably."

Duke Conrad nodded. "Agreed. At that price, your honor will remain unblemished. Moreover, there will be no undue hardships on either side. In a matter of weeks, Constantine will enter Marianstat and receive the crown of Westmark."

"We shall welcome him," said Montmollin. "A Regian king is preferable to a beggar queen. We recognize no boundaries between Regia and Westmark; that is a trivial matter for geographers and toll collectors. We speak the same language, in every sense of the word, barring, of course, our slight differences in accent. Though I must say that your provincial dialects are as incomprehensible as some of ours. My own tenants, among themselves, might as well be jabbering in Trebizonian for all the sense I can make of it.

"Those of our class, however, understand one another very well on both sides of the Domitians," he continued. "Constantine, naturally, appreciates that in Westmark he will be guided by a ruling council: myself, General Erzcour, and some of the higher nobility."

"His Majesty will be grateful for such advisers," Conrad answered. "But now, Baron, I raise a point regarding this council. One of your compatriots was obliged, not long ago, to seek refuge with us. His help has been invaluable. He has shared with us his intimate knowledge of your governmental procedures, the practical workings of your ministries—and other information we have found extremely interesting. He is presently living quietly in Regia, occupied in writing his memoirs."

"They should be fascinating," said Montmollin. "Autobiography suits him. It is the highest form of lying."

"I am sure he could be induced to put aside his literary efforts and sit as a member of your council," said Conrad. "He offers the benefit of long experience in statesmanship. Desirable, you would agree? Certainly, from our point of view, the Sieur De Brussac—"

"Otherwise known as Cabbarus," Montmollin broke in. "I was aware that our former chief minister had chosen Regia for his exile. I did not know he had also chosen a new name."

"He prefers it for the time being."

"Understandably. And the title?"

"We bestowed it on him," admitted Conrad. "A small honor compared with his great assistance to us. For one who was nearly king of Westmark, 'sieur' is not extravagant."

"Cabbarus is unacceptable to us, whatever he calls himself," returned Montmollin. "Under no circumstances will he hold a place in our council. The fellow has less breeding than one of my dogs, and the sensibilities of a hog butcher. He would be worse than a discredit, he would be an embarrassment. A tyrant who gives tyranny a bad name!"

Conrad shrugged. "As you wish. You see, we are not difficult. Now, gentlemen, I propose a toast—"

The duke had only raised his glass when the door flew open. A bright-haired, slender young man in disheveled hunting garb clattered into the room. He smiled at the guests, who immediately came to their feet. The new arrival's face was still rosy from the mountain air. While the downy beginnings of a moustache had sprouted on his narrow upper lip, he had not yet come into the full strength of his ancestral features that looked so well on gold coins. King Constantine IX was sixteen years old.

"I got my stag," said Constantine. "It looks like Erzcour got a ram," he added, noticing the splotches on the general's face. "Congratulations. You can wash now. You needn't go around bloody forever. Have I missed anything?"

"Nothing of consequence," Conrad said.

Ignoring his uncle's frown, Constantine threw himself on a couch and stretched his legs. "We'll have our war, then? Good. It's my first, you know. I'll be in personal command."

"I think not this time," said Conrad. "There will be other opportunities when you have more experience."

"How else am I to get it?"

"Majesty," said Erzcour, "it will be a short campaign, little better than a field exercise."

"All the more reason," said Constantine. "No, uncle, I'm not going to sit in Breslin Palace until it's over. I want to see things for myself."

"We shall talk about it later," said the duke.

"One thing more," said Montmollin. "Regian troops are to be kept firmly in hand. No needless destruction, looting, and all the rest of it."

"Soldiers loot," replied Conrad. "It is a customary amusement."

"Even so, it must not be excessive. Your field officers must be so instructed. It will only work to all our disadvantage if there is ill will between our people and your soldiery."

"Montmollin's right," said Constantine, sitting up. "We're not really enemies, you know."

"We understand that, Connie," the duke said impatiently. "Now, gentlemen, if we have nothing further— Ah, yes. It almost slipped my mind. That young fellow, what's his name—the Sieur De Brussac suggested, quite rightly, that we put him out of the way. The Sieur De Brussac passed along a name to you, did he not, Erzcour? A man he recommended. You have seen to the matter?"

"I have, Your Highness. Since I have not heard otherwise, I assume the affair is settled."

Constantine, meanwhile, had climbed to his feet and gone to the side of Montmollin. "I don't care what they say, I think the war will be a fine thing and I won't be put off it. As far as your queen is concerned, I can see why you want to be rid of her. But wouldn't it be easier if you simply had someone go and do it?"

Montmollin looked askance. "Your Majesty, we are not barbarians."

# 4

The pain in his ribs encouraged him to believe he was still alive. Opening his eyes, he doubted it. A gaunt, white-streaked face loomed over him. The ghostly shape laid a finger on its lips, turned, and disappeared. Theo could not decide whether his mind was playing tricks or whether he had slipped into some netherworld of phantoms, where, having been shot point-blank, he surely belonged.

He sat up cautiously. His wound throbbed under a heavy wrapping of bandages. Pale sunlight washed over the plaster walls. From beyond the window he heard a rushing, bubbling sound, and a constant clatter. Where he was and how he got there interested him less than setting off again as best he could. His clothing was gone, but he noticed a pile of garments on a bench. He hauled himself out of the cot and began awkwardly to dress.

The phantom was back, this time carrying a dish of unmistakably real food. He beckoned to Theo, who realized what had given the man his ghostly appearance was a dusting of flour which seemed to have settled permanently on his face, hair, and clothing. Though flesh and blood, he kept silent as a tomb. When Theo began to fling questions at him, the stranger only eyed him gloomily and answered none of them.

"Impatient to be up? That's a good sign."

Florian had strolled into the room. He wore a faded blue army greatcoat over his shoulders. His elegantly drawn face with its scatter of pockmarks was weather-beaten, grained with fine lines. Hatless, hair loose and uncropped, he stood with his thumbs in his belt while his gray eyes observed Theo's surprise with amusement.

"This is Kopple, the miller. He's a good friend," said Florian as the gaunt man nodded briefly. "No chatterbox, as you may have gathered, which is all to his credit. Go on, eat your breakfast. Slowly, now. You haven't had a solid meal this past week."

Theo stared at him. "I've been here that long?"

"You're lucky to be anywhere for any length of time." Florian took a packet from the table. Theo recognized his journal. A black-rimmed hole had been drilled through the pages.

"We found this in your jacket," Florian said. "It stopped the bullet. Slowed it down, at any rate. That saved your life. Half of it. For the other half"—he held up Theo's sketchbook—"you forgot this at Mull when you went galloping away. Luther set off after you to give it back. He heard the shot, but he was too late to catch whoever did it, and had enough on his hands fishing you out of the Carla. He thought it wise to bring you here. Some of our people around Mull helped him. You had quite a journey—not that you took much notice of it. You'll mend soon."

"Soon isn't soon enough," said Theo. "I should be with Mickle right now. Where is this place?"

"It doesn't matter," said Florian. "You're in no state to travel. Even if you were—"

"I'm going. I have to," Theo broke in. "Mickle's heard nothing from me. She doesn't know what happened or why I'm not there."

"So much the better," said Florian. "If you're worried about that, I'll try to get word to her. She'll know you're alive, which is all she needs to know, and I'll trust her to keep that bit of news to herself."

"Do you mean you won't let me go? I'm not a prisoner." Theo glanced at Florian. "Or am I?"

"Of course not. It's for your own good. Listen to me, youngster. Someone was very eager to get rid of you."

"Believe me," said Theo, "I know that better than anybody. It was a man called Skeit. He used to work for Cabbarus."

"Perhaps he still does," Florian said. "He's working for someone, I'll wager. Fellows like that aren't interested in settling their private scores. They have principles. Like the town hangman, they only kill for a fee. No doubt he's sure he killed you. If he finds he didn't, he'll try again. You're safer dead for a while."

"I'm not going to stay dead the rest of my life."

"I hope not. Luther's off to find out what he can. Something's brewing. We've known that, but we still don't know what it is. There's a lot of different fish being fried and I can't lay hands on any of them. Is Master Cabbarus in it? Does he fit with Erzcour and his friends? It may be. But how?"

"Why did you want Erzcour replaced?" Theo asked as Florian paced the room.

"Luther must have told you. The gallant general and the aristocracy appear to be playing a deep game of their own. Very deep. I can't fathom it."

"And I can't fathom what difference any of it makes to you. The army, the aristocracy—why do you care what they're up to? The more trouble for the monarchy, the better pleased you should be."

Florian halted and looked squarely at Theo. "If I thought it would help our cause, yes. The military and the nobility want more power in government, I can smell that. If they get it, they'll make my work all the harder. That doesn't suit me. I'd be foolish to let my enemy grow stronger."

"Then it all has to do with your advantage," Theo replied bitterly. "It wasn't to help Mickle. Or Torrens. Or me. Once, you told me all men were brothers. Nature's law, you said. Doesn't that include us?"

"You asked much the same at Nierkeeping," Florian said, after a long moment. "I've thought about it ever since. You gave me a fine piece of gristle to chew on. But what's to be done with gristle?"

"Swallow it," said Theo, "or spit it out."

"Yes," Florian said, "but I keep chewing."

"It hasn't changed your mind."

"I do what's needed." Florian's face clouded. He added, half to himself, "Sometimes I question. I question. And I can't answer." He smiled suddenly. "There you see the risk in thinking too carefully. That, fortunately, is not the case with Justin."

"Luther said he was with you."

"He is, but not at the moment. He should be back in a few days. He'll be glad to see you."

"Will he? He nearly got killed that day, because of me. I wouldn't blame him if he held a grudge."

"He doesn't talk about it," said Florian. "As for what he thinks, I don't always know his mind. Things seem to drop into it and disappear.

"My fledgling grows a strong pair of wings," Florian went on. "I had expected him to be an eagle; he's becoming more an avenging angel. In any case, he has a following who worship him like one. I count on him to do well. He has a number of marvelous gifts. One of them should be especially useful—or especially dangerous—to a great many people, and himself into the bargain.

"I suppose," Florian said, at Theo's questioning look, "you might call it charm."

Florian had told him he was not a prisoner. Theo had no cause to disbelieve it. Nevertheless, when he regained strength enough to keep his legs from going off in their own directions and was able to walk outdoors, he noticed that he was rarely alone. If he sunned himself in the millhouse yard, or sat by the stream that turned the slatted wheel, Kopple always loomed close by; or several of Florian's people, strangers to Theo, would find work in the stable, granary, or wherever else he wandered.

He had already decided to set out for Marianstat despite Florian's warning. The air had lost its sharp edge, a pale green mist of new leaves hung over the surrounding woodlands. From what bits of talk he overheard, he calculated the mill to be in the western reaches of the valley. The weather favored him, but the journey would be too long on foot. He began passing more time at the stables, sketchbook in hand, taking a lively interest in drawing horses.

One such afternoon, Florian himself sauntered by and stopped to observe.

"You've a good hand at that," he said, "though I'm not sure what your courtiers and ministers will have to say about a prince who draws pictures.

"There's another matter I've wanted to take up with you," he added, smiling. "You're not as much a monarchist as you had me believe. Not according to what you've written in your journal—what was left of it."

"That's private." Theo reddened. "You had no right—

"True. But some temptations are irresistible and thus perhaps forgivable." Florian grinned at him. "You've set down some disapproving views on the subject, to put it mildly. A delicious irony, wouldn't you say, for a lad about to marry the queen of Westmark?"

"It's not the queen of Westmark I'm going to marry," said Theo, "it's Mickle. And—yes, I think the whole idea of aristocracy is wrong. The injustice of it would be bad enough, but it simply doesn't work.

"When I was a printer's devil, I read an old book by a man called Johannes Jacobus. He said it was only common sense for the nobility, the townsfolk, and the peasantry to join in one grand council where everyone had a voice. The king would rule by their agreement. There wouldn't be only one leader of the council, but three. He called them consuls. No one held power at the expense of the others."

Florian laughed and shook his head. "I read that, too, when I was your age. I thought the idea was marvelous. It only needed unselfishness and goodwill to make it work. Poor old Jacobus. He never understood that power is always at someone's expense; sometimes at the expense of those who try to use it best. I soon found out there were flies in his magic ointment."

"He said people were good by nature," Theo replied. "Ill treatment was what turned some of them wicked. Given a chance, they'd choose justice over injustice, they'd rather be kind than cruel. It's a matter of education."

"Do you believe that?"

"Of course. It's the way I feel, and I'm no different from anyone else—though I used to think so."

"Your modesty is as delightful as your innocence," Florian said. "Do you know what happened to Jacobus? He was hounded from pillar to post until he died in a garret. His book was condemned and publicly burned."

"Blame the judge, then."

"It wasn't a judge," said Florian, "but his own colleagues at Freyborg University. They're the ones who burned his book, and only regretted they couldn't do likewise to him."

Florian broke off. One of his men was calling him, and he left Theo searching for a good reply. Finding none immediately at hand, Theo went back to his sketchbook and his plan, trying to arrange his conscience so that he could steal a friend's horse without reckoning himself a thief.

Crossing the yard next morning, he saw Justin coming out of the stable, a blanket roll over his shoulder, a pistol in his belt. He was leaner and taller than Theo remembered; his fine yellow hair, long and loose in the manner of Florian, had grown still paler, while his complexion had weathered to a dark gold. A heavy scar twisted from his brow to his cheek in a stark white furrow.

Justin's violet-colored eyes widened until they seemed to eat up his whole face. He halted, watching intently for a long moment. Then he broke suddenly into a boyish grin and ran to grasp Theo's hand, showering him with questions and waving aside his answers.

"I have to report to Florian," Justin said hastily. "We'll talk later. But—but this is wonderful! After all this time! Not since Nierkeeping!" His grin widened. "What a glorious day that was, eh? I'll never forget it. My first battle, a real baptism of fire. Yours, too, I think. We were hard pressed, all of us." Justin lowered his voice as if sharing a secret. "I can tell you, I thought it was touch and go for a time. Lucky I was on hand to save you from that officer."

Justin clapped him on the shoulder and strode into the house, leaving Theo to puzzle over his words. In fact, at Nierkeeping, an officer of the garrison had set upon Justin with a saber. Theo himself pulled Justin away as the officer swung up his blade again, and had leveled his pistol, ready to fire. In his nightmares, he still saw Justin, his face a bloody mask, and heard his screams to kill the man. Theo had stood frozen for no more than a heartbeat, but it would have cost Justin's life. It was Florian who brought down the officer with a musket shot. The moment had haunted Theo ever since. Whether conscience or cowardice made him hesitate he had never been able to decide. At the last, Mickle helped Theo drag Justin to safety. The day had not been glorious.

Justin had somehow rearranged his memory, giving himself a hero's role, and had spoken with such conviction and likable eagerness that Theo was nearly persuaded to believe the distorted account wholeheartedly. He suddenly understood something of what Florian had meant by "charm."

After a time, he went back into the millhouse where Justin and Florian sat studying a map, too absorbed to notice him. He was about to leave when he heard hoofbeats clattering into the yard and excited voices.

A moment later, Luther stepped through the doorway. He looked saddle-weary, his face grayish, his cloak mud-caked. Kopple and two of Florian's men followed. With a quick nod to Theo, Luther went directly to Florian.

"There's fighting in the Col. The Regians attacked yesterday, before dawn. I was up there when it started. By now, they'll have a couple of regiments in the valley."

If Florian was taken aback, he showed no sign. He was thoughtful for a moment, then asked, "What do you make of it, Luther? Are they up to some other sort of business? They're foolish if they invade through the passes. Erzcour could hold them off with a corporal's guard."

"Erzcour surrendered," Luther said flatly. "He's ordered all Westmark units to lay down their arms. To save lives and avoid bloodshed in hopeless battle against vastly superior forces—that was his last order of the day. The Regians have him prisoner."

"Why did he surrender?" Theo had been listening in mounting dismay. "If he could have held his ground, why didn't he?"

"It's clear enough. He never intended to," Florian said. "I warned you something was in the wind."

"There's more," said Luther. "Erzcour surrendered, so did most of his officers. The troops didn't. They were betrayed and they know it. So they're still fighting, as best they can, in disobedience to orders. Call it a mutiny, if you like. In any case, it's a hornet's nest up there."

"Bravo, the mutineers!" Florian jumped from the bench and clapped his hands. "That's something our gallant general didn't reckon on."

Luther shook his head. "The Regians are giving them a bad mauling. They've had to fall back, they can't get themselves in any kind of order. One company tried to make a stand. They were cut to ribbons."

"Florian," Theo broke in, "I can't wait. I have to get to Marianstat."

"No way you'll get through," said Luther, "not as things are going now. The valley's crawling with Regians, don't you understand that?"

"Luther is right," Florian added. "You have to put up with us awhile yet." He gave Theo a wry grin. "As for what you've had in mind these past days, it's no use making off with one of our horses. Or were you thinking of taking two?"

"Would you have stopped me?" demanded Theo, abashed that Florian had so easily guessed his secret plan.

"Not then," said Florian. "But I would now. If Skeit doesn't shoot you, the Regians no doubt will."

"What are you going to do?"

"Do? Why, youngster, I don't see that I'm expected

to do anything. I'm sorry. It's a bloody piece of business, but it's between Westmark and Regia. I have no part in it. You forget we're a band of desperate outlaws."

"That's not true," retorted Theo. "King Augustine pardoned you."

"Yes," Florian said, smiling, "but I didn't pardon him."

"You wanted to help us before." Theo pressed on. "I don't care what your reasons were. There must be something your people can do now."

"I was willing to give you fair warning," answered Florian. "For my own advantage, as you quickly pointed out. That was one thing. It cost me nothing. Are you asking me to put my people into the field? As what? Irregular troops? Partisans? That's something different, much more expensive. I'm surprised that you, of all people, should ask it."

"I'm willing," put in Justin. "I can have men and mounts here before the week's out. Do it, Florian. It would be a marvelous chance, better than Nierkeeping. Think how much we could learn from it."

"A costly school." Florian said nothing for a while, pacing the room. He turned to Luther. "What do you think?"

"Fight as irregulars? This comes on us too soon. I'm not sure we're ready."

"Not as ready as I'd like," said Florian. "But Justin has a point. This could be the moment to test our hand. If the army's in disarray, some will join us. A good many, as it might be. We'd come out of it stronger than before."

"Or cut to pieces," Luther said. "And yet—it's a chance too good to miss."

"One thing more." Florian looked sharply at Theo. "It's time you had your first lesson in statecraft, my Prince: Give nothing for nothing. If we do this, we shall want something in return.

"A piece of paper," Florian went on. "I want our freedom spelled out in laws. I want the equality of every man and woman in Westmark; they shall be equal before the law, and the law shall be equal before them. The only privilege I accept is the privilege—no, the right—of making a decent life for ourselves. In short, a constitution. I'll not ask my people to die for anything less."

"I'd give you that without your asking," said Theo. "It isn't up to me. I can't speak for Mickle or Dr. Torrens."

"No, but you can speak for us. I want your word that, come what may, you'll support our cause. Against the aristocracy. Against the monarchy. If need be, against the queen herself. Do I have your promise?"

Florian's gray eyes looked at him steadily. Theo felt Justin and Luther watching him, too. Finally, he nodded. "Yes. You have it."

"Luther, your work is cut out for you," said Florian. "I want Zara here. And Stock. It seems that I'll need all of my children."

# 5

That same morning, a high-wheeled coach rattled over the wooden bridge spanning the Alma, where the river swung north to flow into the larger waters of the Carla. The driver, stubby-legged, a huge cocked hat on the back of his head, a clay pipe between his teeth, coaxed the gray mare to step out briskly, as he hoped to cover the leagues between Carlsbruch and Mull before nightfall. His passengers were a young gentleman from Napolita, Signor Michelo, and his tutor, Professor Lombasso.

Count Las Bombas had first considered posing as a traveling journalist, but finally decided on a more respectable occupation. "This should go down splendidly with the provincials," he told Mickle. "As sightseers, it will be quite natural for us to nose around as much as we please, hear local gossip, inquire about odd happenings—it's part of your education. Besides, tourists who spend money are always welcome."

Mickle's ragamuffin garb had let her slip unremarked through the alleys of Marianstat and join the waiting count. Las Bombas, meanwhile, had acquired garments in keeping with their new roles: for Mickle, clothing of quality befitting a serious young student of good family; for himself, somber professorial robes and a pair of spectacles. He took pains to blotch his fingers with ink and arrange some egg stains on his shirt front, explaining that a measure of scruffiness would enhance his scholarly appearance.

As the count predicted, they were cordially received everywhere. After leaving Marianstat, they stopped briefly at posthouses and inns along the valley road. Without seeming to press for information, they pieced together a fair account of Theo's movements. Mickle was thus able to reason that he was probably in Mull when he heard the news of her father's death. If, in fact, he had started back then, he had disappeared somewhere between there and Carlsbruch. Queen Caroline was wrong. He had not dropped out of sight on purpose. While it relieved her mind to that extent, it increased her fear that he had met with some accident. She was all the more anxious to reach her destination and question the innkeeper.

"Musket will have us there for supper," the count assured her, "if we don't get too badly caught in a thunderstorm. One seems to be on the way."

Mickle, too, had grown aware of distant rumbling, although the sky above them was cloudless. In the direction of Mull hung a gray smudge that quickly darkened, streaking upward to drift over the eastern reaches of the Carla.

Musket, soon after, reined up and halted in the middle of the road. The count put his head out the window, impatient to learn the cause of the delay. Uniformed figures, some on foot, some on horseback, were rapidly bearing down on them.

"The local garrison on field exercises," explained Las Bombas. "Badly turned out, I must say. Someone should mention it to their commanding officer. We'll have to let them by."

Mickle had climbed out of the coach to see for herself. Soldiers they were, but in no military formation. Before she knew what was happening, she found herself amid a tide of grimy faces and jostling bodies. Most carried muskets slung over their shoulders, but a number were weaponless. A few disheveled cavalrymen tried to force their lathered mounts through the press of troops and baggage carts.

Las Bombas hurried to join Mickle. One of the soldiers had seized Friska's reins and was trying to head the mare and coach in the opposite direction.

"What's all this?" cried Las Bombas. "Disgraceful! Form ranks, there! Where's your officer?"

The soldiers within earshot burst into guffaws. A sergeant with a bloody rag tied about his head shouldered his way to the coach. "Get back wherever you came from. The Regians are in Mull."

With half a dozen others shouting at the same time, it took Mickle a few moments to understand what had happened. Las Bombas, too, finally realized that the Regians had not only captured the town but were, as well, already sweeping through the valley.

"Do what the fellow says," he cried, seizing Mickle's arm. "Get clear of this mess, the faster the better. I can't make heads or tails of why it started, but that's the least of our worries. Once you're in Marianstat—"

"The war's here, it isn't in Marianstat," declared

Mickle. "I'm staying. They're my soldiers, aren't they?'

"They're nobody's at this point. Call them soldiers? Great heavens, girl, I've seen better-organized mobs. It's every man for himself here. They don't even have a commanding officer."

"They do now."

Mickle pulled away from the count, flung off her hat and jacket, and clambered to the roof of the coach. She put her fingers between her teeth and blew an ear-shattering whistle. This, coming from what was unmistakably a girl looking down coolly at them, brought most of the troops up short.

The count, seeing no way to stop her, tried to make the best of it. He climbed to the box beside Musket and bawled at the top of his voice, "Attention! Present arms! That's the queen of Westmark!"

His military outburst brought more guffaws and a selection of barrack-room comments.

One trooper shouted up: "Queen, are you, missy? If you're a queen, where's your crown?"

Mickle, seeing he wore a hussar's uniform, grinned at him. "If you're a cavalryman, where's your horse?"

The soldiers, at this, whooped and cheered her, turning the joke on their comrade. Meantime, a bedraggled, hatless figure in an officer's tunic pushed through the crowd.

"Your Majesty!" he cried, saluting. "Beg to report: Captain Witz at your orders!"

The count stared at the officer, a sandy-haired young man whose enormous cavalry-style moustache looked as disarrayed as its owner. "You! Pipsqueak! You're the idiot who tried to arrest us after that business at Nierkeeping!"

"Beg to report, sir, that is correct," the officer replied. "I had no idea then that you were with Queen Augusta—princess, as she was at the time. But I recognize her now, sir, no question about it."

The sergeant who had tried to turn the coach had been studying Mickle in growing amazement. He turned to the milling soldiers and roared, "Get back in ranks, you sorry lot of imbeciles! The captain's right. I saw her when I was in the palace guard. It's the new queen, true as she stands there."

Mickle could not be certain of all that happened afterward; nor could the troopers themselves, when they boasted of it to those who came later. By the time other stragglers arrived, they had already named themselves the Old Guard. The queen, they decided, belonged first and foremost to them; no one else had quite the same right to claim her.

"You should have seen it," said one of them. "A chit of a girl, jawing back and forth with us, cheeky as a bantam rooster. She's got a tongue in her head, too. Better than a mule driver."

Another added, "The Beggar Queen, some call her. Well, I say we could have used more beggars like her in the Col."

At the moment, Mickle was unaware of any of this. Someone, seeing her shivering, had put a cavalry cloak around her shoulders.

When at last she climbed down, the soldiers would have kept on cheering and crowding around her had not Las Bombas pulled her into the relative quiet inside the coach. She beckoned for the sergeant and Witz to join her.

The sergeant she promoted to captain on the spot,

telling him to choose his own under-officers and to put his men into some kind of order.

"You'll be my military adviser," she said to Las Bombas as the former sergeant clambered out. "You should know about these things. Didn't Theo tell me you were in the Salamanca Lancers?"

"Ah—yes, well, that was some time ago," replied the count. "They do things differently these days. But if you want my advice, it's exactly what it was before: Get out in a hurry."

"Beg to report," put in Witz, "I concur with His Excellency. We can't hold against the Regians, not in the state we're in. The disorganization, not to mention the total disregard of military regulations, is shocking. We must have time to regroup, and Your Majesty can be assured the Regians won't give it to us."

"If they won't give it to us, we'll have to take it," said Mickle. "Now, Captain Witz—"

"Your Majesty," broke in Witz, reddening, "in the press of circumstances, I forgot myself. I'm no longer entitled to that rank. When my commanding officer surrendered, he ordered me to do the same. I—I disobeyed. It was the first time in my career that I refused to carry out an order. By regulation, I should be demoted, even shot.

"But, Your Majesty, really it is too bad," he blurted out, almost in tears. "We could have stood our ground. There was no reason to surrender. With all due respect for my superiors, beg to report, they're despicable cowards. But the regulations are quite clear. I was guilty of insubordination, dereliction of duty, and conduct unbecoming an officer."

"Good for you," said Mickle. "Very well, you're not

a captain. You're now a colonel, on my personal staff—as soon as I have one, that is."

"But it's out of the question," Witz protested in morose earnestness. "An officer cannot be promoted without approval of his commanding general—that would be General Erzcour, and he's a prisoner."

"I've just changed the regulations," Mickle said. "You're a colonel and I order you to start behaving like one."

Witz gaped at her, dumbstruck that anyone, even the queen of Westmark, would dare take such a high hand with military regulations. He blushed like a boy, his moustache trembled in admiration.

Military regulations required his loyalty and obedience to his sovereign; they did not require him to fall in love with her.

But he did, then and there, without officially recognizing it; and he was to remain so for the rest of his life.

During the next half hour, Mickle promoted another dozen of the most likely troopers and set them in command of newly formed companies. She charged Musket with collecting what provisions her tattered army had brought and rationing them out fairly among all the detachments. Still wrapped in her cavalry cloak, Witz trotting at her heels, she made her way among the soldiers, inspecting weapons, questioning, joking, until Las Bombas pleaded with her to set off without further delay. To his great relief, she finally agreed. Musket produced a dented bugle from the count's paraphernalia and blared out the signal to retreat.

Colonel Witz had managed to collect a creased and

dog-eared map. Mickle pored over it while the coach led the way back toward Carlsbruch. If they could reach there in time, Witz ventured, they stood some chance of holding it; perhaps long enough for some of the nearby garrisons to join them.

"What about the bridge?" Mickle asked. "The one we crossed this morning. What if we tear it down? Or burn it before the Regians get there? That should stop them for a while."

"I have already considered that," said Witz, who had begun scribbling numbers on a scrap of paper. "From a tactical viewpoint, it would be highly desirable."

"This fellow's a military maniac," Las Bombas muttered. "We're trying to save our necks; he's doing arithmetic."

"Beg to report," said Witz, after several moments, "I've estimated the rate of march, applying the factor of how long it takes one infantryman to pass a given point, the distance between ourselves and the Regian advance column—"

"Next you'll be throwing in laundry lists and phases of the moon!" cried Las Bombas. "To the point, man!"

"It's only routine staff work," replied Witz, looking wounded, "but it must be done, sir. It's part of my duties. Ah—now, according to my calculations, it might just be possible to cross the bridge and destroy it before the Regians overtake us. However, beg to report, several infantry companies will have to remain on the far side. There's no time—"

"Abandon them?" demanded Mickle. "We can't. They'll be killed."

"Presumably." Witz jotted down another row of figures. "At an expected casualty rate of—yes, here we have it, the loss would be nearly total; but, under the circumstances, quite acceptable."

"Not acceptable," returned Mickle. "You find some better numbers, Colonel. I want all my people across that bridge."

Scratching his head and chewing at his moustache, Witz returned to his calculations. He was still in the midst of them when Musket urged Friska over the bridge. Mickle pounded on the coach roof, signaling the dwarf to halt. Before Musket reined up, she had already flung open the door and jumped out. Las Bombas shouted for her to come back and press on to Carlsbruch.

"Witz will take charge. This is his business, not yours."

"I'll go when the bridge is down," Mickle called over her shoulder, "and not before."

She ran to the head of the bridge, Las Bombas fuming and protesting behind her. By the time she reached the middle of the span, the first horsemen had begun galloping across. Seeing Mickle, they burst into cheers and one, dismounting, hoisted her into his saddle. Several of the hussars turned their steeds and rode to her side, taking it on themselves to form the queen's bodyguard, which they continued to be during all the days that followed.

Witz, despairing of his calculations, finally threw his papers into the air and set about doing what he had mathematically proved impossible. As new detachments arrived, he began issuing a spate of orders, sending back gallopers with messages to the rearward companies. As soon as the leading column of foot soldiers appeared, they were set to work hastily gathering twigs and branches and piling them along both sides of the bridge.

Musket had commandeered a saber nearly as long as himself. Brandishing this weapon, he leaped to the wooden railing and scuttled back and forth like a rope dancer, bellowing for the men to hurry. More than the Regians at their heels, the sight of Musket and his gigantic blade spurred them along faster still.

Even Las Bombas, who had never ceased warning Mickle to make all haste for Carlsbruch, threw himself into the work of gathering wood for kindling. His academic robes were begrimed, his plump cheeks flushed and sweat-streaked with his unaccustomed effort.

Witz appeared everywhere at once. As the main body of troops streamed across the bridge, he posted a musket company along the riverbank and another at the bridgehead. "Beg to report," he cried, jubilant, "I think we might pull it off!" Then he dashed away again, shouting for the men who had already crossed to make room for their comrades now racing over the span.

Soon, however, Mickle heard the crackle of musketry from the woodlands on the far side of the Alma. The Regians had caught up with the end of the column and were harassing it sharply. By the time the rear guard came to the bridge, their attackers were already upon them. The companies Witz had stationed at the riverside began firing at the gray green lines of Regian infantry, forcing them to keep their distance and allow the last of Mickle's troops to disengage and retreat across the Alma.

Witz, meantime, had readied two of the baggage carts and loaded each with kegs of gunpowder. These he ordered run out and left in the middle of the bridge. Musket, still perched on the railing, had taken command of a dozen men with torches.

As what seemed the last of the stragglers sped over the bridge, Mickle's shout of triumph turned to a gasp of dismay. The Regians, seeing they could no longer keep all their prey from escaping, turned their musketry on the remnants of a company that had stood their ground to cover their comrades' retreat. The hail of bullets from the Regian line drove these hapless troops away from the bridgehead to the far bank. There, the Regians poured volley after volley. Seeing themselves trapped beyond hope of rescue, some of the Westmark troops flung up their hands in surrender, only to be shot down at the river's edge. Others stripped off their knapsacks and were killed as they plunged into the Alma. The current caught the bodies and sent them spinning against the pilings of the bridge, where the water had taken on a pinkish hue.

Mickle broke away from her bodyguard. Dismounting, she ran to Las Bombas and threw herself on him, sobbing like a child. "Make it stop! Make it stop!"

The count held her a moment, then with deliberate roughness shook her by the shoulders. "You wanted to be a field commander? Be one! You'll see worse before you've done. This time you've come off cheaply."

Mickle, shocked out of her tears, tore herself from the count and ran to the bridge. Shouts of alarm had risen from the troops there. Musket and the torchbearers, setting the brushwood alight, had run to safety as the whole structure seemed to burst into flame. But the fire had only flared, then sank before spreading to the powder kegs. The Regians, withdrawing from what had appeared an impassable blaze but was now burning too slowly, saw the chance to carry the bridge by storm.

Witz, instantly realizing what had happened, snatched a torch and sprinted toward the nearest cart while musket balls from the far bank whistled around him. He sped on to fling his torch into the cart, leaped through the flaming brushwood, and vaulted the railing to plunge headlong into the Alma.

Behind him, the cart exploded in a burst of splinters and a shower of sparks; an instant later, the second cart blew apart. The bridge trembled and lurched sideways into the water.

Mickle scrambled down to the riverbank among her infantry. There was no sign of Witz. In another moment, she glimpsed his head bob up from the current. Ignoring the bullets smacking into the water on all sides of him, he calmly and methodically was swimming for shore. A dozen hands reached to pull him out.

Hair plastered against his head, moustache dripping and tangled with weeds, he shook himself like a water spaniel. Sighting Mickle, he brought himself to sopping attention.

"Your Majesty," cried Witz, as if his pronouncement alone could make it official, "beg to report: The bridge is down!"

# 6

Zara and Stock were the first arrivals. The onetime dressmaker, "the russet divinity" as Florian fondly called her, had cropped her heavy auburn hair and dressed herself in the coarse clothing of a farm laborer. She gave Theo only a brief greeting and a quick, appraising glance of her green eyes, then went to find Florian.

The burly poet, lingering to unsaddle their horses, pumped Theo's hand. "There's great news! I could hardly wait to tell you."

Stock was so flushed with excitement Theo could only suppose the war had suddenly ended. Stock, however, brushed aside any questions before Theo could ask them, threw back his massive head, thrust a hand in the breast of his jacket, and declaimed: "I have the honor and pleasure to announce I have ceased to be an unpublished poet. The children of my fancy have at last emerged from the shadows into the daylight of print."

Theo, as delighted as the poet himself, demanded when it had happened and who had brought them out.

Stock pursed his lips and tugged at the sparse fringe above his brow. The poet was only a few years older than Theo, but had already begun balding: a sore point, since Stock perceived a mystical bond between poetry and hair, and found himself in the contradictory position of being abundant in one and scant in the other.

"Ah—the publisher is myself," replied Stock. "That is to say, The Westmark Phoenix, the press you built for us in Freyborg. Zara turned out to be quite clever with it. She set up the type. I did the heavy work."

"So you finally learned to run the press? Congratulations again."

"I mean that I corrected the proofs." Stock drew out a small volume and pressed it into Theo's hands. "Here, I signed this one for you. No need to read the whole thing right away. Unless, of course, you want to."

Theo glanced at the first few pages. "Why, Stock, these are very fine."

"Not fine! Superb! This one—let me show you. And this—"

From what Theo gathered, while Stock riffled through the slender book, it was a collection of love poems. When he ventured to ask the object of the author's affections, the poet made an expansive gesture.

"The Muse herself, my boy. None other! None more worthy! Though inconstant on occasion she may be, I make her the humble offering of my total devotion. Your true poet needs no flesh-and-blood model. If anything, it distracts. But speaking of devotion, a small surprise is on the way."

Zara was beckoning from the millhouse. Stock broke off and went to join her. Within the hour, Theo learned what the poet had meant. A cart rolled into the yard, and he recognized the driver as Jellinek, the keeper of the Freyborg tavern, stout, red-faced, good-natured as ever; and beside him, a fair-haired girl with a milky complexion: Rina, the golden divinity.

"Luther told me what was afoot," said Jellinek, as Florian came out to see the unexpected arrivals. "I herewith offer my services. You can't fight a war on an empty stomach. You'll need a provisioner, a commissary. I don't promise miracles, but I'll see that none of you starve."

"You mean you've come to poison us all as you did in Freyborg," returned Florian, laughing and clapping the innkeeper on the back. "We survived your cooking then, I've no doubt we'll live through it now. To work with you, old friend. Kopple will show you our stores, such as they are."

Florian was less delighted at the presence of Rina. "I counted on you staying in Freyborg. We must have someone there to keep an eye on things."

"There's plenty of others," Rina protested. "I can do as well as anyone here."

"The best you can do is turn around and go home," said Florian. "If you're needed, I promise to send for you."

The girl's blue eyes were not on Florian, but on Justin, who had come out of the millhouse. In Freyborg, Theo recalled, both Zara and Rina had been clearly in love with Florian. Zara, he sensed, had not changed her feelings, which he guessed to be as sharp and fierce as they had been. Now, however, Rina, the dreamily sentimental laundress, watched only Justin.

"Let her stay," Justin urged, not unaware of Rina's gaze. "She can be with my people. She won't be the only woman, there should be half a dozen others."

"She'll have saddle sores the first hour," put in Zara. "Rina, you've no business here, you'll only be underfoot."

Before any squabble broke out, Florian raised his hand. "On further consideration, it occurs to me that our golden divinity may be useful. Her profession could prove an advantage."

"I'm not scrubbing clothes," Rina declared. "I didn't come for that."

"Laundry it may be, but not what you suppose," Florian said. He motioned for them to follow him inside, adding to Theo, "You should sit in our council of war, too. We won't bar a future prince. You'll get your wish, by the way. Luther should be with us by the end of the week. We'll know better how things stand, and we'll get you to Marianstat one way or another. You can explain to your queen what we intend to do."

Relieved at learning he would soon be on his way, Theo found a place beside Stock at the table. Florian called them to silence. In a light, almost bantering tone, he welcomed his children, and for a moment Theo had the impression Florian had invited them only to take part in some complex but amusing game. Quickly, however, his manner turned more serious. His gray eyes studied each face as he spoke quietly of their plans. It was not a Florian that Theo had seen before, even at Nierkeeping. There was a new and different air of authority about him that gripped each listener. If Florian had ever questioned or doubted himself, as he had admitted to Theo, he showed no sign of it. Even Stock, notorious for his constant and exuberant interruptions, kept silent.

As Theo expected, Florian was to be commander-in-chief, with Zara his second-in-command. They, with Jellinek, would leave the mill and travel west in the direction of Belvitsa, where Florian would make his headquarters, putting himself in touch with his own people and the Westmark detachments in that region.

"Luther is on his way back from there," said Florian. "He should bring good news. With luck, we'll be more than irregulars; we may have a whole army of our own.

"Luther will be our eyes and ears," Florian went on. "We've already agreed that he's to keep us abreast of one another's doings. You'll very likely see more of him than of me; but his orders are to be followed as if they were mine."

This last was directed to Justin, who was to lead his troop into the Domitians, on the south bank of the Carla. "The Regians will be advancing," said Florian. "Let them. The farther they go, the more their supply lines will stretch thin. Attack them, harry them, nip their flanks, give them no rest. You're to fight no pitched battles, though. If you do, they'll cut you to pieces. You're a wolf pack, not a regiment of dragoons."

Justin nodded agreement, though he appeared disappointed. Florian named Stock as Justin's second-in-command, then turned his attention to Rina.

"The weapons of our golden divinity will be soap and washboard. But in a special way. She will offer to work for the Regians, in the occupied villages nearest to where Justin is operating. She must watch and listen, and learn all she can of our enemy's plans and strength. Who would think of distrusting a laundress, above all such a charming one? I count on her cleverness to find means of sending out word."

Rina beamed and blushed, enchanted to be useful to Justin. Having finished his business and promising to speak again later with each of them, Florian ended the council. "Now," he declared, "I trust Jellinek is putting up a farewell feast. Next time we are all together, it will be a victory banquet."

Stock jumped to his feet. "What about our names? We must each have a *nom de guerre.*"

"There speaks the romantic poet," said Florian. "Call yourself what you please, my valiant versifier, as long as you do your work. For the rest of us—"

"Stock, for once, might have a sensible idea," put in Zara. "It might be wiser if our real names weren't known."

Florian thought for a moment. "There's something to be said for it, at that. Very well, I leave the choice to our poet."

"To begin," said Stock, "I offer Florian the noblest of falcons: Peregrine." He bowed to Zara. "And to our russet divinity, the dauntless dragon: Firedrake.

"For Luther, what more fitting than the bird of wisdom and bearer of tidings to the gods themselves? Raven.

"Our laundress can surely be nothing but Lapwing, the bird that feigns injury to mislead its enemies.

"To Justin, I propose the fierce butcher-bird: Shrike. And for myself, I claim the legendary creature that rises from its own ashes—and which also happens to be the ensign under which my poems are available to an eager public: Phoenix."

Stock, having gone red in the face as a consequence of his oration, sat down looking vastly pleased with himself. His companions cheered and clapped their hands, reminding Theo more of their boisterous gatherings in Jellinek's tavern than a solemn council of war. He also felt left out, as he did in those days when he longed to be called one of Florian's children. Now, though he told himself it was foolish, he admitted he would have been better pleased if Stock had included him. He insisted it made no difference.

He could not deny that it did.

He saw little of Florian during the next few days. Luther still had not come back. Given no duties, Theo consoled himself with his sketches, gaining the admiration of Stock, who came from time to time to look over his shoulder. Although the poet gave pride of place to his own muse, judging all others beneath her, he granted Theo a certain talent; Theo's praise of his poems, in addition, did not make Stock unkindly disposed toward a fellow artist.

Justin, promising a dozen men and mounts, proved better than his word. Before the week was out, nearly twice the number had arrived at Kopple's mill. Jellinek was hard pressed to feed them all, and Kopple unable to shelter so many. The newcomers made camp in the fringe of woods near the stream.

Some Theo recognized as former students from Freyborg; others were hardly more than boys who, clearly, had never handled a firearm in their lives. All were devoted to Justin. Theo could read it in their faces as Justin, who spent most of his time in the camp, walked among them, calling each by name, showing one how to load a musket, another how to attack with a saber. He brightened at each new arrival; as his troop increased, including three or four young women, he grew almost radiant. Theo tried to sketch him, without success.

"You're seeing him as our old friend Justin," declared Stock. "You'll never catch him that way. You must see him now as something quite different, say a young Jove—if you can imagine Jove ever being young, but you take my meaning. Or perhaps Phoebus Apollo would be closer to it."

Although Stock had been named second-in-command, Justin relied more often on one of the older men of his company, a lanky trooper with a wide, snaggle-toothed grin in a face covered with a stubble of beard. His long arms and sloping shoulders had won him the affectionate nickname of the Monkey, which he took good-naturedly and with a measure of pride. As nimble and shrewd as his namesake, with a store of jokes and comical songs, the Monkey had become the company favorite. By wordless agreement, he undertook the training of the new arrivals, with a combination of browbeating and cajolery, half clown, half drillmaster.

Nothing was beyond the Monkey's skill. He could mend harness leathers, take apart a musket, sew as well as a seamstress, and cook better than Jellinek. At saber practice, which he organized to keep his comrades occupied, he was a strong opponent.

During one such exercise, when for once he was getting the worst of it, he gave ground, stumbled, and dropped the point of his blade. His young adversary, afraid the Monkey had hurt himself, drew back and lowered his guard. The Monkey scuttled forward, swinging his blade up in a backhanded stroke.

The trooper was suddenly asprawl on the turf, with the Monkey's boot on his saber arm and the Monkey's point at his throat. Chuckling, the Monkey helped the bewildered boy to his feet.

"A dirty trick," said Stock. "He didn't learn that in a fencing academy. That fellow's done some soldiering. Cavalry, I'd guess, from that pigeon-toed walk of his."

"What's a regular doing here?" asked Theo.

The poet shrugged. "Who cares? He's a gem. Justin's lucky to have him."

With Florian and Zara caught up in their own preparations, and Luther still absent, Theo spent more of his time in the camp. If Justin's company had any inkling who he was, it made no difference to them. Justin, too, welcomed Theo and was delighted for him to see how they had improved. They would be ready to leave by the next day.

"Marvelous, aren't they?" he said to Theo. "I'd trust any one of them with my life. The best part is that they're here because they want to be. They're not conscripts in some royal army, being flogged into battle. They'll fight for what they believe in: for justice, brotherhood, a decent life. That's your true nobility: the people, not your perfumed aristocrats."

"A company of knights and paladins!" cried Stock. "I'll compose an epic for you."

"Don't joke about it, Stock," returned Justin. He

looked at Theo. "You believe in the same things. Florian knows that; so do I. But I understand why you'd rather be in Marianstat. None of us thinks any the less of you for it. You'll help us in your own way. You're quite right, you'll be safer there."

"I never said anything about my safety." Theo reddened. Justin had spoken without malice, but his words had stung.

"I don't mean that I hold it against you," Justin went on. "We can only do our best, whatever it may be. Your work is very likely as important as ours, and suits you better. I can't say I envy you. I'd find court life despicable. But that's the difference between us, isn't it?"

Justin put out his hand. "I'll say farewell to you now, in case I don't see you tomorrow. We'll be leaving early."

"Farewell—" The idea had been in his mind for days. Until now, he had put it aside with a dozen reasons why it was out of the question. His reasons suddenly lost their force. As a printer's devil, he had lived out his life through books. Yet part of him had been unsatisfied and restless; that part had been larger than he had imagined. He had taken up with Las Bombas for the adventure of it, he could not deny that. The count's purposes had been rather less than noble, and Theo had quit him. Florian's cause was not only noble, but one Theo believed in and longed to be a part of.

All that held him back was his love for Mickle. Many of Justin's people had left their sweethearts, loving them no less. That he should turn from doing as much struck him as selfish, even contemptible. Mickle did not need him as much as he needed her. He had not proved himself as his own man, and if he went to her now he would never know if he was worthy of her.

Justin had turned away. Theo called after him. "Wait—suppose I wanted to go with you?"

Justin smiled and shook his head. "I'm surprised you ask. It's hardly your kind of work." His violet eyes narrowed as he studied Theo for a long moment. His scar seemed to darken and move with a life of its own. "You should know that by now. Especially after Nierkeeping."

Theo felt as if he had been struck. Justin suddenly broke into his boyish grin. "It's not that I wouldn't be glad to have you along. I just don't see what help you'd be."

"Theo's clever with a pencil," Stock put in. "He could turn his hand to mapmaking. And a few lessons from the admirable Monkey should make him a scout for us. There's plenty for him to do."

"That might well be," said Justin. "Yes, Stock, I'd be glad for extra hands. It's up to Florian, though. He's the one to decide."

"He's your commander, not mine," said Theo. "My decisions are my own."

He left the camp and went back to the house. Florian, too busy to give him more than a moment's hearing, dismissed the idea out of hand. "I want you in Marianstat. I won't have you risking your neck in what doesn't concern you."

Still hoping he could change Florian's mind, Theo resolved to talk with him again. When Stock saw the frown on Theo's face, the poet easily guessed what had happened.

"I'm sorry," said Stock. "If I had my way, you'd be with us. Justin feels the same. But I'm afraid it's too late, in any case. Justin's decided not to wait until tomorrow. We're to pack up and leave now. Some of his people have already started; they'll set Rina on her way. The rest of us had better stir ourselves. Otherwise, our young Apollo will be highly displeased."

Florian and Zara came to take only brief leave of Justin and his company and returned to their own work. The camp was suddenly empty, with hardly a sign it had ever been occupied. Theo did not go back to the house, but stayed alone even after the last of the riders had disappeared.

When, finally, he turned away, he heard a rustling through the undergrowth. The Monkey had ridden up, leading one of the remounts.

The Monkey gestured at the empty-saddled horse. "From the captain. He said to tell you he'd never keep anyone from a second chance. He said you'd know."

"Does he mean—?"

The Monkey gave him a lopsided wink. "That's all. She's a good beast. What you do—well, that's your business, isn't it?"

Theo glanced back toward the house. The sketchbook and remains of his journal were there. The Monkey had already turned his mount and started through the woods. Theo called after him to wait. The Monkey did not halt.

Theo ran to the mare and swung into the saddle.

# PART II
# THE MONKEY

# 7

Weasel sat cross-legged on the rim of the fountain. He was usually delighted to spend afternoons in Great Augustine Square observing the passing crowd. At the moment, however, he was in a reflective, philosophical frame of mind.

"Sparrow," he said, "I've been wondering."

The girl beside him kicked her bare heels against the stones. Like her younger brother, she wore a shapeless garment of sacking. Her legs were long and spindly, her knees like a pair of clenched fists. She did not answer, her attention engaged by a street accident between a coach and a peddler's cart. Seeing no fatalities or noteworthy injuries, she finally lost interest and turned her pointed, foxy face to Weasel, giving him the superior, indulgent look of one too knowledgeable to wonder about anything.

Weasel pursued his speculation. "What do you want to be when you grow up?"

"I'm grown up now."

"Are not," said Weasel. "You hardly got your bosoms."

Sparrow tossed her head. "That's all you know."

"I know what I want to be." Weasel hesitated, bashful at revealing his life's goal even to his sister. His dream, nevertheless, was too grand to keep to himself. His eyes fixed on some distant, invisible star, his voice was hushed by the awesomeness of his ambition. "If I worked hard, Sparrow, if I truly studied at it, I know I could do it. I could be a thief."

"You?" Sparrow snorted. That Weasel should fancy himself worthy of entering the exalted company of thieves was overweening pride that required correction. She considered smacking him. Instead, she expressed her doubt by a loud blast through her pursed lips.

"I'm better than you think," retorted Weasel, indignant at having exposed his golden secret to sisterly scorn. "You don't know it, but I've been practicing. I'll be a fine thief."

"Begging's the trade for you," said Sparrow in a practical tone, hoping to make him see reason. "You'd do well at it, especially if you don't grow any more."

Weasel pushed out his lower lip. He looked on the verge of tears. Sparrow, fearing she might have been a little harsh, tried to console him. "You'd like it, once you learned. I'm not saying you'd match the cripples and peg legs—though there's always hope for you. But you could manage with sores and scabs. Really, it's almost as good as thieving."

"No." Weasel puffed out his chest; the inflation made no visible difference to his birdcage of ribs. "I'm clever enough to be a thief right now. Even a pickpocket."

This added audacity made Sparrow gasp. Within the

high calling of thievery, she revered pickpockets as the uppermost nobility.

"You watch." Weasel unfolded himself and slid from his perch. He strode toward the accident, where the carter and the coachman still argued. The prosperous-looking occupant of the coach had stepped out to examine his vehicle for damage.

Sparrow, exasperated, started after her brother. Weasel slipped through the onlookers and was jostling closer to the owner of the coach. Weasel, Sparrow admitted, showed natural skill. Even her sharp eyes could not catch the movement of his hand toward the gentleman's waistcoat.

Weasel, however, was not quite as expert as he had boasted. At the last moment, he fumbled, and his hand came back empty. Realizing his failure, he tried to dart away. His intended victim moved faster. He seized Weasel by the arm, shook him furiously, and began shouting for a constable.

Sparrow, seeing that the struggling Weasel could not pull free, flung herself on her brother's captor and set about kicking him in the shins. Tough though they were, Sparrow's bare toes produced little effect against her opponent's boots. She, too, was gripped and held.

Two constables had arrived. Hearing enough of the gentleman's account to learn on which side justice lay, they collared both urchins and, not without difficulty, hauled them through the crowd.

"Keller! Keller!" Sparrow had glimpsed a familiar face among the bystanders.

The man to whom Sparrow so desperately appealed was youngish, with a full crop of tousled chestnut hair.

His usual expression was one of ironic amusement, but at sight of the prisoners he blinked in happy surprise and hurried to Sparrow's side.

The constables, like the rest of the onlookers, recognized him immediately. Keller was known all over Marianstat as the publisher of the comic journal, *Old Kasperl*. His presence was greeted with cheers and boisterous laughter, and a number of shouted comments that were more affectionate than polite.

When Keller demanded the facts of the matter, so many voices chimed in that the journalist held his head with one hand and waved them to silence with the other.

"I've heard all I need," Keller announced. "The case is clear, open and shut." He gestured toward the owner of the coach, whose scowl did not place him among *Old Kasperl*'s devoted readers. "Quite obviously, on the very face of it, this suspicious-looking fellow has attempted to assault and rob two upstanding young citizens, and our brave constables are protecting them from further onslaught. Shame on you, sir! If you must commit felonies, choose someone your own size. Really, sir, you criminals are starting to behave like the aristocracy."

"Damn you and your tomfoolery," the man retorted. "One tried to pick my pocket. The other attacked me. These officers will do their duty, and no more of your stupid nonsense."

"Do you mean I've got it wrong way round?" Keller feigned bewilderment. "My dear sir, forgive me. I misunderstood. Wait—I have it now. *They* were the ones who robbed and attacked *you*?

"But this is all very puzzling," Keller went on. "From

the way this young lady is hopping on one leg, I conclude that her toe sustained more damage than your boot. I call that assault by deadly footwear, with intent to bunion: a grave offense. Now, as to loss of property— What, there was none? Then I suggest, sir, you have caused this diligent young gentleman to waste his time. And time, you must agree, is extremely valuable. I'm afraid this deplorable affair will cost you dear. I urge you to drop the whole business."

Applause from the onlookers convinced the would-be plaintiff that while he might have the law on his side, he could not say as much for the crowd. Even the constables chuckled and nudged each other. He motioned angrily for them to unhand their prisoners. "Go to the devil, the lot of you."

"I, for one, most assuredly will," replied Keller.

Taking Sparrow and Weasel in tow, the journalist led them across the square. "Water rats, I'm glad to see you. But why did you leave your fens and marshes? Marianstat, I admit, is something of a swamp, but not such an agreeable one."

"We live here now," said Sparrow.

"Ah? And where, pray tell, is your town residence? Château Underbridge?"

"Never heard of it," said Weasel. "We sleep in doorways. Not as good as our hut. But Sparrow wanted to leave. There used to be all sorts of good things we could fish out of the river, but our pickings started getting thin."

"Times are bad everywhere," said Keller. "Even for scavengers."

"Besides," added Weasel, "later there was constables

and soldiers poking around. They even came in boats. It was all we could do to keep out of their way."

"Too bad," said Keller. "They were looking for you."

"Why?" Sparrow asked. "What did we do wrong?"

"Nothing. You did right," said Keller. "You generously offered me hospitality when I had certain difficulties of my own with the law. We wanted to find you and properly reward you—I and that other gentleman you rescued."

"Who, the white-haired old buffer? The one floating in the river with his arm cut up?"

Keller nodded. "The white-haired old buffer, as you so aptly describe him, is alive and well, thanks to you. He has a new trade. He is none other than the queen's chief minister."

Sparrow was unimpressed. "What's the reward?"

"Do we get money?" Weasel chimed in.

"In the case of high state officials," Keller said, "a reward more commonly takes the form of sincere thanks. Sometimes a gold watch. For my part, I intend to give you something better than mere cash. I propose to offer you a life."

"Got one," said Weasel.

"This will be brand-new. I've been thinking a great deal about you two since we parted."

Sparrow perked up. No one, to her recollection, had ever admitted thinking about her. She looked at the journalist with new interest.

"You shall lodge with me," said Keller. "You shall be fed and clothed. I need a couple extra pairs of feet. You shall run the occasional errand and otherwise make yourselves useful. As you scavenged the river, you shall learn to scavenge the town: for scraps of news, rags of humorous incidents, shreds of gossip, and all such fascinating rubbish.

"In the course of time, if you prove sufficiently impudent, enterprising, inquisitive, and generally disreputable—and you are well on the way—you yourselves might become scriveners."

"Is that as good as a thief?" asked Weasel.

"Better," said Keller. "It's thievery of the highest degree. We steal people's lives, thoughts, feelings, and sell them. Some of us even steal each other's ideas, but that's rather frowned on; we try to maintain a sort of honor."

Weasel's face lit up. "I like that."

"And you, my dear young lady? Is that what you might want to be?"

Sparrow thought for a moment. "What I mostly want to be is warm. But I guess scrivening will do."

Keller occupied apartments above the offices of *Old Kasperl,* and it was there he brought his new colleagues, putting them first in the hands of Madam Bertha, his long-suffering housekeeper. The good woman was predictably aghast at the journalist's latest and, in her opinion, greatest folly. She ticked off on her fingers the disasters sure to follow. She had reached only eight of them, including arson and assassination, when Keller interrupted.

"Don't forget the worst. I intend teaching them to read and write. The consequences will surely prove horrendous."

Madam Bertha suggested that if Keller applied in his personal life half the good sense he put into his journal, he would be better off.

"Ah, my dear Madam Bertha," said Keller, "that's the

way of it, don't you see? I only write *Old Kasperl,* I never read it."

Making a show of aggravation and disapproval, grumbling that Keller would bring about the ruin of them all, and thereby trying to conceal her fondness for the journalist, the old woman herded the protesting Sparrow and Weasel off to be scrubbed and put into what clean clothing she could find.

Keller, meantime, went down to his office and sent the printer's devil with a note to Dr. Torrens, advising that their benefactors had been discovered at last. The journalist and the physician had grown to be friends since their suffering at the hands of Cabbarus; Keller was a regular visitor at the Juliana Palace. Only recently, Torrens had confided that the queen had gone off on a madcap search for Theo. He trusted the journalist not to reveal this. Keller, though dismayed at keeping such astounding news out of his journal, reluctantly agreed when Torrens reminded him he was speaking to him privately as a friend. The chief minister's purpose had been to enlist Keller's help in tracing the queen. To this Keller also agreed, but his efforts had so far been unsuccessful.

On that same afternoon, word of the invasion reached Marianstat, and the news that Queen Augusta had taken personal command of the army. The Marianstatters had poured into the streets, not in alarm but in celebration. A minor engagement at an obscure bridge was already being hailed as the Victory of Alma, setting the populace in joyful frenzy. The insolent Regians had been taught a sharp lesson; the valiant troops of Westmark and their queen would soon send the villains packing.

Keller stood in his doorway, observing the throng. He was, apparently, the only one who had taken pains to consult a map. It did not need a field marshal to see that if the Regians ever forced a crossing, if they advanced in any kind of strength, they would be a dagger pointed at the capital itself. He smelled a disaster in the making.

"My poor fools," Keller murmured, as the happy crowd swirled past. "My poor dear fools."

Some of the revelers called him to join them. Keller turned away.

His business was to point out folly, not drown in it.

Under the circumstances, Keller did not expect to hear from Torrens, the chief minister having more on his mind than a pair of water rats. The journalist was, therefore, surprised when only a few days later he and his charges were summoned to the Juliana, and a royal carriage arrived to carry them there.

Sparrow and Weasel hardly batted an eye at their visit to a palace, looking on it simply as a house bigger and better furnished but draftier than their hut on the riverbank. They were more than happy to see the white-haired old buffer again, but less than grateful for the gold watches he presented to them. Queen Caroline herself received the water rats in her apartments and made much of them, as if the presence of children consoled her for the absence of her daughter. She had cups of chocolate brought for the pair, which endeared her to Sparrow and Weasel forever.

Torrens, meanwhile, talked apart with the journalist behind the closed doors of the ministerial offices. The physician looked haggard. The defection of many field officers had left the army in disarray, and he had ordered the formation of local militias. He agreed with Keller. The kingdom stood in greater danger than even the cabinet ministers realized.

"To make matters worse," Torrens said, "Queen Augusta has very unwisely put herself in the thick of it; exactly where, I do not yet know. It was pointless of her to run off as she did. An unsigned note has come into my hands, claiming Theo is safe. If only she had waited—"

"And yet," said Keller, "it may be for the best. She's become the darling of the Marianstatters."

"For how long, if things go badly? Aside from that, this came to my attention some days ago. In the normal course, I would have thrown it out. Now I cannot ignore it. If this is circulated and believed, it may do irreparable harm."

He handed the journalist a pamphlet, badly printed on coarse paper. "I disregard the personal attack on me. I have been attacked before. This vicious slander strikes at Queen Caroline, at Queen Augusta, at the future prince consort— I have never seen anything as foul and contemptible as this offal. The insinuations, the barefaced lies—"

Keller glanced at the text. "I give the author credit for a colorful imagination."

"It is despicable trash," said Torrens. "Worse, appearing now of all times."

"Despicable," said Keller, "but only trash; low journalism that stops short of high treason."

"But no less dangerous. We have learned the name of the scribbler who wrote it and the printer who published it. The minister of justice has drawn up warrants for their arrest. Here, too, is a decree forbidding publication of offensive material. And, for the protection of honest writers, licenses will henceforth be required, and granted only after careful investigation. The papers await my signature of approval."

"Which, of course, you won't give," said Keller. "How can you? My dear Torrens, you and I have often talked about these things. You yourself have said the press must not be muzzled. I can't imagine you'd even consider it."

"I must consider it now," replied Torrens. "Desperate conditions require desperate remedies."

"Even to following the example of your predecessor?"

"Cabbarus forbade the truth," Torrens answered. "I would forbid only lies."

"To my knowledge," said Keller, "no one in the history of the world has managed that."

"This will not hinder any decent, reasonable journalist," Torrens went on. "On the contrary, it would allow more freedom."

"Allow more by taking some away?" put in Keller. "My dear friend, you know that one thing leads to another. You may well end by censoring cookbooks for giving indigestion. Suppose, one day, Old Kasperl in all good conscience might make certain comments found to be, shall we say, less than amusing?"

"You have answered your own question. That makes the difference: in good conscience."

"I didn't know you had the gift of reading a man's conscience," Keller said. "My profoundest admiration."

Their talk grew more heated until Keller, who had

always prided himself on keeping an amused detachment, found his own temper starting to fray, though it was clear to him Torrens was speaking more in anguish than anger. The journalist thought it best to end the conversation before it turned into a quarrel.

"I've been delighted to give my opinion," said Keller, "if not my agreement."

Torrens did not answer. Keller said no more, but collected his water rats and took his leave.

After the journalist had gone, Torrens sat down at his desk and put his head in his hands. He preferred the practice of medicine to the practice of statecraft. He had accepted his position with greatest reluctance. He understood the ills of the body and their cures. Statesmanship, he thought bitterly, was a disease without a cure, and he had been afflicted with it, for the sake of the kingdom.

He signed the papers.

# 8

Justin's company had made camp for the night when Theo and the Monkey caught up with them. Justin did not appear surprised at Theo's arrival, seeming to take it for granted. When Theo tried to thank him for sending the mare, Justin shook his head as if he had forgotten about it. He told Theo to settle himself where he pleased; the Monkey would see to blankets and whatever gear he needed. Theo found a place near the horse lines. Stock joined him soon after.

"I imagined you'd be along," said the poet, who had saved a share of his evening ration. "Decent of Justin, wasn't it? But you ought to know I'm the one who thought of the horse."

Theo gratefully munched the heel of black bread. The sky was brighter than he had ever seen it, and the night almost warm. The woods gave off an overpowering smell of moist earth and moldering leaves. He did not speculate on what Florian would do after realizing he was gone, he was too satisfied by his own decision.

Stock lay at ease on the turf, hands under his head,

one leg cocked over his bent knee. "The Muse, I am happy to report, has favored me with a visit. I have it all in my head, it's only a question of setting it down when I have the chance. Justin's kept us on the go today. He's very keen—as we all are. He thought I was joking about knights and paladins. I wasn't. There's a spirit. You'll catch it once you're here awhile. Everyone's behaved wonderfully; the women have set us all an example."

The poet sat up and leaned on an elbow. "Did you ever wonder if things could have been different? How much of it's accident? I mean, if you hadn't happened to run into Queen Augusta when you did— Is it true she was going about in rags, without any notion who she was? Remarkable.

"And the business about Cabbarus. The word is you actually had the rascal's life in your hands; you kept him from tumbling off a tower and cracking his skull."

"It was something like that."

Stock laughed. "Then, my lad, you have much to answer for. Justin thinks, and I agree with him, that Cabbarus must have a finger in this Regian thing. What if you'd let him drop? Do you think any of the rest would have happened? Would we be here now? You might say it's all your doing."

"I don't know," said Theo. "Sometimes I wonder the same thing, and if I did right. One way or another, I suppose I'm to blame."

"Or to thank. Imagine what an experience this will be. For me, at any rate. How am I to be a poet if I don't see a few things for myself? How are you to be an artist?"

"I doubt that I will."

"Ah—that's right. You'll be a prince. I forgot. It's not likely one can do both. Then again, why not?" Stock climbed to his feet. "I'm off to inspect the guard posts. You'll have a turn, we all do. There's probably not a Regian within miles. The Monkey guesses they're all on the south bank of the Carla. Still, we must take care."

Stock disappeared into the underbrush. Theo wished the poet had said nothing of Mickle. He had been trying not to think of that part of his life and, until then, had done well enough. By the time he was able to close his eyes, it was dawn. The Monkey was already up and rousing the company.

The next days were dazzling blue and sun-dappled. Justin was making his way generally eastward but gradually bearing toward the Carla River. He set his riders a good pace to make up for the heavily overgrown stretches that forced all to dismount and walk their horses. The Monkey brought up the rear, urging on anyone who showed signs of straggling.

If Theo had sensed any coolness when he joined the troop, it had vanished. He was even invited to the meetings Justin held at the beginning and end of each day with Stock, the Monkey, two of the Freyborg students, and a dark-haired girl named Rosana. These were Justin's staff officers and, as Theo realized, his closest and most devoted comrades. Theo was flattered, though Justin never asked his opinion or gave him any duties.

Theo had begun to suppose that he was not seriously counted part of the company. One day, however, after they had borne south for a distance, Justin ordered Theo and the Monkey to scout ahead and map likely fording places across the Carla. A simple task, but it made Theo feel that Justin had bestowed some priceless gift. Despite his misgivings and questions of ill will between them, Theo was eager for Justin's approval. Or, at least, his forgiveness.

With the Monkey's help, he reached the Carla before midday. They found several fording places. The Monkey, flat on his belly behind a screen of brush, squinted through a spyglass and pointed out the best. Theo set about drawing a detailed map. He admired and envied the Monkey's skill as a scout; the Monkey, in turn, was impressed by Theo's ability as a mapmaker. By the time they returned to camp, they had struck up an easygoing comradeship.

Justin was sitting under a tree, Stock and his other officers around him. Theo hurried to report his success. Another man squatted beside Justin. It was Luther.

"The wise Raven has flown to us with great tidings—" began Stock, but left off at a glance from Justin. The gray-haired man was looking at Theo with the expression of a professor who has caught a favorite student in a dangerous prank.

"Luther has splendid news for us," Justin said. "You'll be especially interested."

Luther repeated what he had told the others: that Queen Augusta had taken command of troops at the Alma. How she had come to be there in the first place he had no idea. Her troops had very sensibly fallen back to Carlsbruch. Luther had not seen her, but intended making his way there with messages from Florian.

Theo, listening amazed, nearly forgot the map. He hastily put it in Justin's hands. Luther motioned him apart.

"I won't say if you're a fool or not." Luther stopped a few paces from Justin and the others, who were poring over Theo's work. "If I'd reached the mill a day sooner— Florian, by the way, isn't very pleased at what you've done."

"I don't see it's any of his concern."

"He does. I'm to bring you to Carlsbruch. What's the frown? That should make you happy, since your girl's there."

"Yes, I'd have wanted—but not now. Luther, don't you see I can't? Yes, I want to be with Mickle. That's not the point. I can't let that make any difference. Justin did a fine thing, letting me join—"

"Florian isn't overjoyed about that, either," broke in Luther. "Justin can manage without you."

"That's still not the point. Don't you understand? For once, I'm doing something worthwhile, something I believe in. Really doing, not just talking about it. If I go to Carlsbruch, what then? To be on a staff of some kind? Do you think Mickle's officers would give me any real work to do? I'd be no more than the prince consort. Not even that. Only the future prince consort."

"That's for you to settle," said Luther. "Pack up, lad."

"No. If Mickle were in my place, she'd do the same. I don't care if Florian's unhappy. I'm not one of his people. He can't order me."

"But I can order Justin to send you away."

Theo looked squarely at him. "You won't, though. If you were going to, you'd have done it already. You know I'm right to stay."

"You're the only one who knows that."

"When you're in Carlsbruch, will you give Mickle a letter? I'll write it now, you'll have it before you go."

"No letters," Luther said. "I want no papers on me if I have the bad luck to be captured. But I'll pass along a message."

"Say that you've seen me and explain why I'm here. She'll understand. Say I love her. As she knows."

Luther nodded. "Good-bye, then. I expect I'll be back, one day or another."

"I never thanked you for saving my life."

"No need. See that you hang on to it."

That night, after Luther had gone, they forded the Carla. Justin, taking advantage of the darkness, pressed on without a halt into the wide belt of woodland skirting the Domitians. By morning, they had made camp in the towering shadow of the Horngard. Much to the relief of Stock, who had been thoroughly soaked during the crossing, Justin ordered a rest. Theo had hardly stretched out when, to his surprise, Justin called all officers to him.

The Monkey and a few others, who had followed later as a rear guard, had galloped into the clearing. They had sighted Regians a little way downriver.

"It's only a quartermaster company." The Monkey spat through his teeth. "Cooks and clerks. A handful of infantry for escort—old crocks, mostly, who should have been mustered out long ago. They've got some nice cartloads of stores: grain, fodder, some rations for Mull, I'd guess."

Justin was delighted at the news, but added, "We can still rest a bit. If they're following the road, we'll catch them up easily enough."

"I don't think so, Captain," said the Monkey. "As I

see it, they're trying to join a column that's outmarched them. We don't know who's following them, either. If you've any mind to gobble them, you do it now."

"Hay and oats?" put in Stock. "Not much of a prize."

"Ah, but there is," the Monkey said. "Powder and shot, too. And the best for last. They've got a light fieldpiece, a trim little popgun for one of their mountain batteries."

"Cannon?" Justin sprang to his feet, eyes alight.

The Monkey grinned enormously. "Yours for the taking."

"We'll have it, then," cried Justin, clapping his hands. "We'll have it, and everything else."

As word of the planned attack ran through the camp, the company suddenly forgot their weariness. There was feverish haste to make ready. Theo's face tingled. Stock was grinning and chuckling to himself. The tired horses turned frisky, whinnying and curvetting as Justin signaled the riders to move out.

Justin had given his orders quickly and clearly. As the company bore closer to the road, they divided into three groups: the first two, led by Justin and the Monkey, would launch the attack. The third, under Stock's command, would hold back until the engagement had well begun, then gallop in to seize the supplies. Justin and the Monkey would deal with the cannon. The action was to take place with all speed, the company doing its work and withdrawing before the Regians could regain their balance.

Theo had been ordered to Stock's party. The poet, grumbling that he was to be no more than a teamster and ration handler, could hardly curb his horse, let alone his impatience, while the others pressed on. Theo's heart pounded, he felt giddy. It seemed he had been waiting, frozen in his saddle, for hours. Nevertheless, when the firing began, it came as a shock. He startled and galloped after Stock, who had plunged ahead.

Without remembering how he got there, Theo found himself scrambling through billows of smoke. Justin's and the Monkey's riders had taken the company in the midst of preparing their midday meal. Two tall cook pots had been overturned; their contents, what looked like a gray stew, spilled across the ground. The mess sergeant, who vaguely reminded Theo of Jellinek, an apron around his belly, was shouting and waving his arms, a look of utter bewilderment on his red face.

Someone had untethered the packhorses. Theo seized the first sack of provisions he saw and hauled it to the troopers hastily loading the animals. Two of the carts had been set on fire. The Regian infantrymen, tunics unbuttoned, barely had time to snatch their muskets. Of Justin's party, those still mounted were plunging their horses amid the terrified foot soldiers. Theo, drenched with sweat, had lost sight of Stock but glimpsed Justin and the Monkey at the cannon.

It was bigger than Theo had imagined from the Monkey's offhanded description, with a black iron barrel and heavy breech. It was hooked to a light, high-wheeled limber. Some of Justin's people were straining to swing it around and drag it clear.

Stock suddenly reappeared, yelling for Theo to give a hand with a powder keg. When he glanced back, Theo saw that the cook, puffing and gasping, and half a dozen of his quartermaster comrades had been pressed into hauling away their own gun. With the Monkey flailing at them with the flat of his saber, the Regians had been obliged to seize the shaft of the limber and do the work of the horses, which were now loaded with bundles of stores.

Stock, remounted, bawled for Theo. The burdened pack animals had started up the slope into the woodland. Theo kicked his heels into the mare's flanks. His eyes smarted with the smoke from the burning carts, the reek of gunpowder clung to him even after Stock's party had left the Regian company far behind.

The poet, in his flush of exuberance at the success of their first engagement, had led them far out of their way. He refused, nevertheless, to admit he was lost.

"Military tactics!" he cried, gleeful at how much they had managed to carry off. "Go back the same way we came? Never! Confuse the enemy—even more than they are now!"

Stock continued in high spirits, congratulating himself and his men. Theo, no less excited, could guess that the poet already had in mind the glorious report he would deliver. Finally, after a number of wrong turns and much backtracking, they reached the camp. Justin and the rest of the company had arrived long before.

There was a festive air about the camp. The Monkey perched triumphantly on the limber. Justin, who had been examining the cannon, ran to meet them. He did not reproach Stock for his tardiness, but only urged him and Theo to come and admire the prize.

"A beauty!" Justin cried. "The Monkey can teach us how to aim and fire. You've got powder and shot? Wonderful! You did splendidly, all of you. Not a man lost. I wish Florian could have seen us.

"And the Regians, having to steal their own gun!

They pulled it all the way, the hardest work those fellows have ever done, I should think."

"Where are they?" asked Theo, while Justin led them to the cannon, eager to show how it worked and looking as if he were about to load and fire it then and there.

"Who? Oh—the Regians," Justin said. "I had them shot."

# 9

Sparrow was in love. She had never been in that condition before; she did not realize she was in it now. She simply took it for granted, as natural as rain or sun. She envied Madam Bertha, who prepared Keller's meals and constantly chided him for not eating enough of them, for staying out till all hours, for neglecting his health and his laundry. Instead of resenting the housekeeper, Sparrow imitated her. Madam Bertha could not withstand such unintended flattery. She took Sparrow to her heart, deciding that anyone so concerned for the journalist would probably not burn down the house or steal the spoons.

Keller, who had other things on his mind, was unaware of all this. He was merely pleased they got on so well.

Weasel, in his own fashion, worshiped Keller and offered his greatest gift: He renounced all ambition to become a thief, and put his mind to his lessons.

As for those, Sparrow learned faster than her brother. What pride she took in her accomplishments she kept to herself. She preferred to give the impression that letters were small things she could have grasped on her own, had she wanted, and did so now only because Keller set great store by them. Weasel, however, was continually wonder-struck. Also, he believed Keller had invented the alphabet.

Weasel, like his sister, dogged his benefactor's footsteps. He adopted Keller's ambling gait as best he could. He would have been happy to curl up and sleep the night at Keller's door, but Madam Bertha did not allow it.

During the day, Sparrow and Weasel ran errands. They remembered Keller had spoken of scavenging the town for scraps of gossip, which they did gladly. They found great quantity but little variety. The townsfolk talked of nothing but the war. The flush of the Alma victory persisted. New troops mustered daily in Great Augustine Square to the rattle of drums and the waving of banners. The recruits wore flowers in their buttonholes or in their hats; some put the blossoms into their musket muzzles.

The pair observed this, bright-eyed with delight. Neither had seen anything like it. Weasel found it especially stirring, but a little puzzling.

Finally, his curiosity got the better of him and he asked his sister, "What's a war?"

"How can you be so stupid?" said Sparrow. "Everybody knows that."

"Well, I do know," retorted Weasel. "I forgot."

Sparrow gave a sigh of long-suffering. It was her duty, nevertheless, to instruct her brother from time to time. "What it is, mostly, is marching."

Weasel was unsatisfied. "Why would they do that?"

"To get where they want to go, of course."

"Yes, but then what?"

Sparrow thought for a moment, as if recalling all other wars she had seen. "Do you remember the other day, when Keller took us to the park, and Madam Bertha packed our food in a basket?"

"And Keller drank the whole bottle of wine?" Weasel smiled at the pleasant recollection. "That wasn't a war. That was a picnic."

"It's almost the same," replied Sparrow, "only bigger. They go marching off, and carry their food with them. When they get hungry, they stop and eat. Oh—first, they dress up in their uniforms. Then, they meet the enemy."

"I know that part of it," Weasel said proudly. "That's the Regians. Everybody's talking about them. They're cowardly swine and vile wretches. What I don't see is—if they're swine and wretches, why does anybody want anything to do with them?"

"Because they came sneaking in where they don't belong," said Sparrow. "Our soldiers go and fight them and chase them off. That's why they have muskets, to shoot at them. The Regians try to do the same. But they're such cowards, they can't. Then, after they're chased off, everybody marches back and that's the end of it."

"How long will it take?"

Sparrow frowned. "I heard a lot say no time at all. But Keller was talking in the office, and he said the devil of a while."

"Keller's always right."

"Yes. The devil of a while—I guess he means two weeks, maybe three."

"That long?" The boy whistled. Sparrow might as well

have spoken of infinity. He tried to absorb it and gave up. Something intrigued him further.

"The muskets," he said eagerly. "What a racket they'll make! I'd like to be there when they're shooting. But—don't they hurt each other?"

"Of course not," said Sparrow. "At least not if they can help it. Little nit! Do you think they're as stupid as you?"

Keller wanted to see Torrens. They had parted, last time, with a strain of coolness. Keller did not expect much welcome at the Juliana. It was necessary, even so, to speak with the chief minister. The journalist formally requested an audience and was a little surprised when it was readily granted.

Torrens appeared more careworn than before. There were dark blotches under his eyes. Keller had prepared himself for a reception chilly at best. Torrens, however, treated the journalist with consideration and seemed half apologetic. The man, Keller guessed, was ashamed of himself. The chief minister said nothing about their past conversation, his concern was entirely with the war.

"Queen Augusta still holds Carlsbruch," he told Keller. "She hopes to fortify it, according to the reports she sends us. In fact, she is handling her forces with remarkable skill."

"She can't hold forever," said Keller. "The Regians must force her hand sooner or later."

"I fear so. I have no idea of her future plans, but I confess I see no happy outcome. Queen Caroline is frantic, she has sent message after message, and so have I. Augusta refuses to come back. If the Regians overrun her position while she remains there, I dread the consequences. It would be tragedy enough if she were killed in battle. If she were taken prisoner, I would still fear for her life."

"Surely our uninvited guests would observe the rules of war," said Keller, "at least as far as they apply to royalty."

"I am not so confident," said Torrens. "I have since learned, beyond question, that Baron Montmollin and certain others, including General Erzcour, deliberately betrayed us. They wish the queen deposed. Trying to set right old abuses, putting justice before privilege, she has committed the one unpardonable sin: She has threatened their power. They would be better pleased, I daresay, if she did not survive at all. It would simplify matters for them considerably. The Regians would no doubt be glad to oblige."

Keller was tempted to remark that the greed and selfishness of the aristocracy had done worse damage to the kingdom than the insults of any scurrilous pamphleteer. He bit his tongue and let the chief minister go on.

"Something alarms me further," said Torrens. "This is for your ears only, though it is only a matter of time before it becomes public knowledge. Our old friend Florian is fishing in troubled waters. He has taken to the field. A number of our people, especially in the countryside, are joining him. Apparently, he supports the queen—at the moment. If she suffers any serious reverse, I cannot trust him to continue to do so. I respect the man himself; in some ways he is even admirable. But he will seize whatever opportunity comes to hand. He would be a fool if he did not. Whatever else he may be, Master Florian is no fool. He and his followers must be dealt with firmly."

"You are too much in the palace," Keller said. "What you tell me is already public knowledge. I can only warn you, if you treat Florian as an enemy, you'll make matters worse. You can hardly afford more enemies than you already have."

"Those are my concerns," Torrens said. "I will not burden you with them. Forgive me. I presume you have your own."

"Otherwise, I wouldn't have asked to see you? Yes, you're right. Naturally, I'm here to beg a favor."

"You need not beg," said Torrens. "If it is within my power—"

"It is."

"And within my conscience."

"Even that."

"Then," said Torrens, "consider it granted."

The journalist and the chief minister talked awhile, then Keller left for his office. He did not go directly, but strolled around the city. It was a lovely day. By the time he returned to his apartments, Sparrow and Weasel had come back from their own ramblings. Keller sat them down in front of him.

"Water rats," he said, "you are fortunate. Not only do you have the prospect of a brilliant career—I was about to say 'enviable' but that would be stretching things a little—you have also gained the grace and favor of the white-haired old buffer."

"He already gave us watches," said Sparrow.

"Mine doesn't work," added Weasel. "I don't care. I don't know how to tell time."

"He has awarded you something of more substance,"

Keller said. "He has agreed that henceforth you will receive a stipend from the royal purse."

"What's a stipend?" Sparrow asked.

"Money. An allowance, you might say. You will receive it at regular intervals. The finance minister will see to the details, so you needn't trouble yourselves counting on your fingers. You will not be rich. The generosity of the crown does not go quite that far. Nevertheless, water rats, you will be well-off."

"We've always been well-off," said Sparrow.

"Yes, but now you'll be better off. So shall I. For I admit to certain hesitations and misgivings which are now laid to rest.

"I have a debt," Keller went on. "Not a debt of cash. In our profession, that would be ordinary, and the only extraordinary thing would be to pay it. This, however, is a debt of a different nature. Call it a debt of honor: the costliest, which we scribblers can seldom afford. It calls for payment, though payment has never been requested.

"Some while ago, a certain gentleman did me a service, not unlike the one you did. He offered protection when I needed it rather badly. Better, he offered me the use of a printing press, which I needed still more, in a town called Freyborg. As things turned out, I did not have to stay there long, and was able to return here. Nevertheless, the offer was made and accepted. Now, this gentleman, I believe, would be glad for any help that might come his way."

"Who is it?" asked Sparrow. "The white-haired old buffer?"

"Neither white-haired nor old. His name is Florian."

"I've heard of him," Sparrow said. "People were arguing in the square. One said he was a dangerous hothead, another said he was a caution, the very devil of a fellow."

"Correct on all counts," said Keller. "That's neither here nor there. Now that I'm sure you'll be looked after, come what may, I intend to pay what I owe him. Against all reason and common sense, against all my principles and better judgment, I have decided to go off to the war. I expect no difficulty finding my creditor if I look in the right places. Whatever happens, with Madam Bertha on one hand and the old buffer on the other, you have nothing to worry about. I only urge you to behave yourselves, at least to the extent of your abilities. In the case of Weasel, this includes using a handkerchief instead of his fingers. I shall leave tonight. This kind of folly, if done at all, should be done promptly."

Keller had braced himself for an outburst. Sparrow and Weasel sat silent, watching him with round eyes. The journalist felt a twinge of disappointment. Had they protested, wept, or pleaded, he might even have possibly reconsidered.

He did not understand two things: first, that Weasel envied his going on such a splendid outing but stood in too much awe of him to say anything; second, that Sparrow was so devastated as to be dumbstruck.

He did not hear the girl sobbing later in her room.

The water rats had taken a hard blow. However, they had not survived a life in the swamps for nothing. Keller had been gone only two days when Sparrow realized there had been a terrible misunderstanding.

"He was in such a hurry, he forgot," she said. "He's always forgetting something. Madam Bertha told me once he even forgot to uncork a bottle before he poured it. Madam Bertha says he'd go out without his head if he didn't have it attached to his neck."

"Do you think he forgot something this time?"

"Of course he did," said Sparrow. "The most important thing of all."

"Underwear? Keller thinks underwear is important."

"No. He forgot to ask us to go with him."

"That's right!" Weasel's eyes lit up. "He never said a word about it." On reflection, his face fell. "He told us to stay here."

"That shows how much you remember," said Sparrow. "He told us to behave ourselves. That was all. He didn't say how. Keller likes us to figure out such things for ourselves. Now, if Florian helped him, and he's going to help Florian— Keller helped us, so he must have expected us to help him."

"Do you think so?" asked Weasel, hope returning.

"I know it," Sparrow declared.

Weasel recognized only two laws. The second was Keller; the first, Sparrow. "We'd better hurry, then. We don't want to keep him waiting."

Madam Bertha was so distraught over her employer's latest and greatest example of lunacy that she did not immediately notice the absence of the water rats. It was only at the end of the day and well past suppertime that she realized they had gone. She noticed a loaf of bread and a cold fowl absent along with them. The only consolation for her added tears was the knowledge that she had been right about them from the start: They were a pair of thieves.

By then, Sparrow and Weasel were on their way out of the city. Their first problem was to determine where Keller had gone. Sparrow settled it easily by approaching a guard at the Vespera bridge.

"Pardon me, sir," she said politely, "but how do we find the war?"

# 10

The Monkey was grinning at him. Theo went to Justin. "You had the prisoners shot? Why not say you had them murdered?"

Instead of answering, Justin took Theo's arm and drew him to a canvas shelter that had been slung between two trees.

"I didn't want to, you know," Justin said patiently, with no trace of anger in his voice. Had Justin stormed at him, Theo would have been taken less aback. "I had to."

"Cooks and quartermasters! They weren't combat soldiers, they weren't fighting back."

"That's true, they weren't," Justin said. "They weren't fools, either. They saw our camp. They saw how many we are and how well armed. Turn them loose and let them report to their officer? I'd have put every one of my people at risk. Including you."

"You could have kept them prisoners."

"To be fed? Guarded? To be a drag on us?" Justin said. "It was my responsibility. My decision. You tell me one thing: What reasonable choice did I have?"

Theo did not answer. Justin went on. "Then I'll tell you one thing. I'm sorry we left any Regians alive. They know we're here now. They were bound to, sooner or later; I'd have preferred later. Well, no way around that. The Monkey says we should move out before dawn tomorrow, go further up-country and lie low a few days."

Justin pressed his hands against his forehead. "It couldn't be helped. Get some rest. We're tired, all of us.

"Another thing," Justin added, as Theo was about to leave. "If you ever have in mind to question a decision, do it in private." He raised his head and smiled abruptly. "Best yet, don't do it at all."

Stock was sitting on the ground, scratching the turf with the point of his knife. He hardly glanced up when Theo joined him and told him what Justin had said.

"It's sickening," answered the poet, with none of his usual exuberance. "The worst part of it is he's right. At least, I think he is. What would you have done?"

"That's another worst part of it. I don't know."

"The only thing I'm glad of," said Stock, "is that it wasn't up to me. Anyhow, it's over and done. No matter how you look at it, though, there's no honor in it."

"And if the same thing happens again? Suppose you're the one who's ordered to do it?" Theo put the question to Stock only to avoid putting it to himself. He wondered if he should have gone with Luther.

"What I think," the poet said, his balding brow in deep furrows, "is that it's Justin's command. I don't know if he has to answer to us for what he does. But we have to answer to ourselves for what we do. I should have spoken up along with you."

"It wouldn't have helped anything."

"Only my conscience," replied Stock. "You expect certain things in war. You have to swallow them. But how much has to be swallowed? Not all of it, surely. There must be limits. It's a matter of finding them."

Stock said no more. The Monkey was good-naturedly chivvying the company to put the captured supplies in order. Justin had gone back to studying his cannon.

They broke camp next day. It was the first of several moves they were to make before the Monkey found a site in the uplands that he judged safe enough. Theo, by then, could have slept soundly in the midst of the Regian army. His muscles screamed at the constant packing and unpacking of stores. Stock looked ready to drop. Neither dared complain, for Justin worked harder than any of his troop. He took a hand in hitching the horses to the limber and put his own shoulder to the wheel when the gun carriage foundered in the bed of a stream.

Justin treated the cannon like a marvelous new toy. He constantly tinkered with it and almost resented anyone else handling the fieldpiece. The Monkey had chosen several of the troop to serve as gunners, but Justin himself demanded to learn how to aim, load, and fire. He also devised a lighter carriage for the weapon, so it could be brought faster into action.

Even with the cannon, Justin never repeated his first easy success. The Regians, aware now of their enemy, took more pains to arm their supply columns. The provisions the company relied on, both to use for themselves as well as to deprive the Regians, were hard won and harder fought for.

The first deaths came late in the spring. Justin, hoping to replenish his dwindling provisions at one stroke, launched an attack on a lightly defended supply train. Stock and Theo, as usual, waited in reserve for Justin's signal to charge and ransack the disarrayed line.

Before they could do so, a company of Regian infantry burst from the woods on their flank. By the time Stock's party realized the Regians had set a trap for them, it was hopeless to wheel and face their ambushers. Under the volley of musket fire, one of the horses toppled, screaming and kicking its legs. Theo sprang down and pulled the rider free. Stock shouted to fall back. At the same time, the Monkey and his detachment came scrambling up the slope in full retreat. Justin, fortunately, had set his cannon a little distance above them on the brow of a low hill. The fieldpiece flung shot after shot, as fast as the gunners could reload, against the Regian countercharge. Even at that, the gun itself narrowly escaped capture. The Regians did not press their advantage, perhaps fearing they would, in turn, be ambushed in the unfamiliar hills.

Three of the raiding party had been killed outright. Another had taken a musket ball in the chest. The Monkey had flung him across his saddle and had managed to bring him back to the camp. Theo helped the Monkey carry him into Justin's tent, and only then recognized him as the one, hardly more than a boy, who had nearly beaten the Monkey at saber play.

They put him on the ground. Justin knelt beside him. The boy could hardly speak for shock and for the clotted foam welling into his throat. He kept rolling his eyes from side to side, staring at one face and another as if asking to be assured nothing serious had happened to him. He was clearly beyond help.

Theo noticed the Monkey had taken the pistol from his belt and was glancing at Justin. Seeming not to understand, Justin looked blankly at him a moment, then shook his head.

The Monkey shrugged and put away his pistol.

The boy did not die until afternoon.

Early in the morning, two days later, one of the lookouts led in a half-grown girl. She had come from the town lower in the valley. Her knees were scratched, her skirt ripped by brambles. She had been clambering through the brush a good part of the night. She would speak to no one but Captain Shrike.

Justin, already long awake, came out of his tent. Theo, Stock, and most of the company gathered around, watching as the girl went straight to him.

"You're Shrike."

"Am I?" Justin smiled playfully and bent a little, hands on his knees. "Now, missy, what makes you think so?"

With a finger, the girl traced a line across her forehead and down her cheek. She had a round, solemn little face. "I'm to tell you something. The laundress in our town, she wants me to say: from Lapwing."

Stock chuckled, recognizing the name he had bestowed on Rina. He whispered to Theo, "Our golden divinity has been at work for us."

"Oh—I'm to give you this, too." The girl reached into her bodice and handed Justin a square of paper. Justin unfolded it and glanced at it. He laughed and handed it to Theo.

"You taught us to do better work than this in Freyborg."

It was, Theo saw, a poster badly printed on a large, coarse sheet, the ink a little smudged, still not quite dry. Justin took it back and held it up before the company.

"We've given the Regians something to chew on," he declared proudly. "They value our work. Here—a splendid reward for 'help in the capture of bandits.' Hardly a flattering term, but no matter. If they'll pay that much for our heads, we must have nipped them sharply. They're smarting from it."

"There were six hanged yesterday," the girl said, "on account of the fighting. The tailor, the cooper—"

"They had no part in it," Theo burst out. "They weren't our people."

"The Regians called it—reprisal," the girl said. "To pay back for what you did."

"What else from Lapwing?" Justin broke in. His face was impassive.

The girl looked upward a moment, as if recalling a lesson she had learned by heart. She repeated Rina's message in a schoolroom singsong, halting now and again, taking pains to be correct. Lapwing warned Shrike that the Regians planned to send a strong force into the hills. Shrike and his friends must move farther west immediately. Lapwing would be gone by the time her message arrived. She was going toward Eschbach. She would send word again as soon as she could.

The girl stopped and looked around for approval of her recitation. Justin nodded and patted her head. "Well done. But how did you know where to find us?"

The girl gave a sly smile. "We know these parts. Some of us keep an eye on you. We knew when you came. But it's all right. No one told. Not even when the Regians hanged them."

Justin offered to send one of the company partway back with the girl to make sure of her safety. She refused indignantly and set off through the brush before Justin could thank her. He turned to Theo, with a peculiar half-smile.

"You called me a murderer for executing enemy soldiers. What would you call the Regians' killing innocent civilians?"

Theo turned away. He was both ashamed and frightened at himself.

For an instant, he was glad, wildly glad, that Justin had shot the prisoners.

Stock was composing what he assured Theo would be the noblest and most heartfelt work of his career.

"An epic poem," he declared, "which I shall title: *The Saga of Roast Mutton.* It will be in six courses—I mean cantos—and it will feed our spirits, if not our bellies. Even art, my boy, has its limitations."

"You write it," said Theo, with a dour grin. "I'll draw pictures to go with it." He had, in fact, sketched nothing since leaving the mill. It already seemed another age, remote and only half-remembered. Odd, he found, that now of all times he should miss doing it.

"Short of everything else," the poet said, when Theo asked for an explanation of this feeling, "we turn to the Muse for ethereal sustenance of our common clay." He shook his head. "I don't know. Justin doesn't have a muse and it doesn't seem to bother him. No doubt Mars runs a better kitchen than Calliope."

They were all hungry, though Stock suffered most from it. The company had become victims of their own success. In the weeks following Rina's message and their hasty move westward, Justin's operations had gone beyond his best hopes. He and the Monkey had worked out a new plan of action.

"Florian said we must be a wolf pack." Justin had called his officers together as soon as they had settled, for the moment, in the heavy woodlands some leagues above Eschbach. "So we shall be," he added, "but not a single pack. Several."

Now, instead of attacking in full force, Justin divided the company into raiding parties of three or four. Nights, he sent them by turn to harry the Regian columns, roving the valley, striking where least expected. Their targets were not the soldiery but the packhorses and draft animals, which they maimed or hamstrung. The Monkey explained that the loss of a horse or mule caused more damage than the loss of a man.

The raiders, unable to carry off large amounts of provisions, settled for putting the torch to the wagons or slashing open food sacks and scattering the contents. They brought back, when possible, fodder for their own animals, powder and shot for their weapons; the forays seldom allowed them time to lay hands on rations for themselves.

Justin was delighted; his only disappointment, the shortage of ammunition for his cannon. The fieldpiece now stood unused in the camp. The company, however, suffered no serious casualties.

The Regian detachments, by way of reply, took their own measures. Deprived of army stores, foraging parties scoured the countryside, stripping villages and farms of food and livestock. Failing to check Justin's raids, they continued their reprisals. Villagers were hanged or shot, their bodies left as warnings.

The company, as a result, increased its numbers as men and women fled the villages and came to join them. Justin welcomed them, declaring that the Regians had become his best recruiting officers.

The more he added to his troop, however, the more mouths there were to feed. The Monkey, in charge of the rations, doled them out like a miser with his gold. Justin was always on hand when his people were fed, but he touched none of his portion until the others had eaten. Once, a bitter argument broke out between the Monkey and one of the new arrivals, who claimed the Monkey had given a larger share to Rosana. The two men had come close to blows when Justin strode up. They fell silent immediately.

"If you're that hungry," Justin said to the protester, "here, put this in your belly and hold your tongue." He handed his own ration to the man. "We fight Regians, not each other. Remember that. Or, next time," he added flatly, "I'll hang you."

"I wouldn't mind hanging—temporarily," Stock later told Theo. "It might keep me from wanting to swallow something. Tightening my belt doesn't answer. Tightening my gullet might help."

Justin had sent the two of them that night to hold one of the outposts. Stock grumbled at not going with a raiding party.

"At least it would keep my mind off my dinner. Or the lack of it."

The poet was too gloomy even to amuse himself with his saga. "You're lucky, being an artist. You can draw yourself a feast, then stand back and admire it; whereas all I can do is think about it."

Theo put a finger to his lips. He had heard a rustling in the underbrush. Stock readied his musket, then heaved a sigh of relief. It was only the Monkey. The man, Theo realized, had not come from the direction of the camp.

"I could have shot you for a Regian," said the poet. "You rascal, what have you been up to?"

Theo noticed that the Monkey carried a sack under his arm. Hunger had sharpened not only Theo's appetite but his sense of smell. Stock, too, was sniffing like a foxhound.

"I fancied a little walk along the bottomland," said the Monkey. He opened the sack. "You're good fellows. I don't mind going shares, though I did all the work for it. Here, it's a gift from one of the farms. A chicken, some eggs, bread and cheese—"

"Gift?" retorted Theo. "That's most of a week's food for them."

"They'd have given it gladly," said the Monkey, winking, "if I'd waked them up to ask. We're fighting their war for them, aren't we? Fair's fair. It can sit better in my belly than anywhere else."

"You stole it," returned Stock. "That's despicable, Monkey. No, don't worry. I won't say anything to Justin. Not this time."

"Captain's a fine officer," said the Monkey. "He takes

good care of us, but once in a while we have to take care of ourselves."

"Go back to camp," said Stock. "Stuff yourself if you like, so long as I don't have to watch you do it."

The Monkey delved into his sack and brought out a handful of food. "Here, just among the three of us."

"Go to the devil," said Stock. "I don't want any part of your stealing. I'd be as much a thief as you."

Theo left them abruptly and walked a little distance into the brush. The smell of the food had been unbearable. Stock had been right to refuse. He admired the poet for it; he did not trust himself.

He expected the Monkey to be gone when he came back. The Monkey was still there, squatting on a hummock, the sack between his feet. The poet sheepishly wiped the crumbs from his mouth.

"Plenty left," said the Monkey.

Theo bit his lips. Stock said nothing. Theo turned to the Monkey.

"Give it here."

# 11

The guard raised his musket. "Keep off the bridge. Nobody crosses without papers. Do you have any? You might be a couple of Regian spies for all I know. In which case: Bang, bang! And that's the end of you."

Sparrow had no interest in spies or papers. She asked again where to find the war.

The guard thought himself a witty sort of fellow. Being questioned by a pair of young fools who were no danger to him, he decided to amuse himself at their expense; sentry duty was a boring occupation. He scratched his chin.

"That depends on which you're looking for."

"Is there more than one?" asked Sparrow.

"You don't suppose we'd go to all this trouble if there wasn't."

"The biggest, then," said Sparrow. "The best."

"Ah, well, there's a fine big one this very moment between some of my company and a pack of tavern scroungers. You drop in at the King's Crown, you'll find all the war you'd ever want. Tell them I sent you."

Sparrow took Weasel's arm and hustled him off in

the direction of the port. "He doesn't know anything about the war. Not even where it is."

"Keller does go to taverns a lot," suggested Weasel.

"No. That guard was a blockhead. That's why they left him behind."

"Good. It serves him right," said Weasel. "I stole his watch."

Sparrow halted long enough to give Weasel a shaking. "Wretch! You're not to be a thief anymore. Shame on you. What would Keller say?"

"I only did it," complained Weasel, "in case Keller wanted to know what time it was."

The port was home ground to the pair. The former water rats knew every dock and landing stage. Weasel forgot his reprimand and sniffed the portside reek with delight. Sparrow pressed on, leading him to one of the smaller piers, where several rowboats bobbed on the eddies. Sunset had thrown the pier into shadow. Sparrow glanced around. Satisfied she was unobserved, she ordered Weasel into the first boat, untied the mooring line, and jumped after him.

"What are you doing?" cried Weasel.

"Crossing the river, what do you think?" replied Sparrow, bending to the oars. "The war's got to be over there somewhere. That fool might try to shoot us if we go by the bridge. This way's easier."

"You're stealing," Weasel said indignantly. "After what you told me."

"I'm not," said Sparrow. "Didn't you hear the speech in the square the other day? We all have to make sacrifices. Whoever owns this boat is making a sacrifice. I'm helping him do it."

With that, Sparrow doubled her efforts at the oars.

Leaving the craft on the other side of the Vespera, the two trudged eastward until well past nightfall, sometimes following a road, sometimes cutting across the fields. Sparrow's plan was simple: to keep the straightest line possible, confident it would lead sooner or later to Keller. After a few hours, however, Weasel turned cranky, protesting that his feet and belly both ached. Sparrow was also hungry. She had calculated that the food from Madam Bertha's larder would easily tide them over a couple of days. She and Weasel ate it all at one sitting.

"Never mind," said Sparrow. "That makes less we have to carry."

They slept the rest of the night under a hedge. In the morning they were lucky enough to get a ride in a cart and, soon after, unlucky enough to be discovered by the driver, who unpatriotically chased them off.

For the next few days, they fared reasonably well, except for Weasel's blisters. Barns, woodsheds, stables existed for the purpose of sheltering them. Sparrow gave her brother temporary permission to commandeer whatever victuals he found unattended.

"It's not really stealing," Sparrow assured him. "It's to help us get to the war."

"I don't understand," said Weasel, nevertheless glad to oblige. "Stealing is stealing."

Sparrow did not deign to answer.

The following day, they discovered the army. So Sparrow judged from the field of white canvas tents. She had never seen so many horses and wagons; or so many uniformed men, for the most part doing nothing comprehensible. She ran to the nearest, a bearded fellow with a pipe between his teeth. He was sitting on a keg, his tunic undone, his bare feet stretched out in front of him. He was busy greasing his boots. He wore sergeant's insignia, which meant nothing to Sparrow. She strode up to him.

"Where's Keller?"

"Keller who?" The sergeant eyed her. "And who are you? Where the devil did you come from?"

"Keller," Sparrow insisted. "Everyone in Marianstat knows him."

"That's a good reason I never heard of him, since I'm not from Marianstat."

"Are you going to the war?"

The sergeant grimaced. "No way out of it, is there?"

Sparrow was amazed that he seemed less than eager, but she had her own business to attend.

"Where's Florian, then? Keller's with him."

"Florian?" exclaimed the sergeant. "You keep clear of that one. He's a caution."

"That's what everybody says."

"He may be right, he may be wrong. It's no affair of mine, I do what I'm told. But he's got half the countryside stirred up. It wouldn't surprise me too much if we ended fighting him instead of the Regians. You get home, wherever that is. You leave the war to us."

The presence of two young people in camp had drawn the amused attention of the rest of the platoon. They crowded around Sparrow and Weasel as if they were remarkable curiosities. The soldiers offered them food, which Sparrow carefully put away. One of them produced a drum and a pair of sticks and showed Weasel how to beat a tattoo.

Weasel was aglow. One of the men set a cap on Weasel's head, which thrilled him all the more. He rattled away at the drum. The soldiers laughed and told him he could stay and be their drummer. For the briefest moment, Weasel's allegiance was sorely tried.

"Do you think," he ventured to ask Sparrow, "we could stop here awhile? We'll find Keller afterwards."

Sparrow was not lured by uniforms or drums. She finally pulled Weasel away, and they set off again. By day's end, she realized she had come into possession of a secret she had no intention of sharing with her brother. Had she been in the maze of inlets at the mouth of the Vespera, she could have navigated eyes shut. Now, out of her element, she admitted to herself what she dared not admit to Weasel: She had no idea where she was going.

Keller had looked in the right places, not expecting the right places to be so easily found. Florian's activities and whereabouts were no longer hidden. The journalist, leaving Marianstat, had invested in a horse, not wishing to rely on public coaches. After little more than a week, it would have cost him much effort not to find Florian's headquarters, near Altus-Birkenfeld on the south side of the Vespera.

Florian, in a weather-stained blue greatcoat, was at a field desk in front of his tent when Keller was escorted to him. Several officers sat with him; the journalist recognized only the auburn-haired young woman, Zara.

Florian greeted him warmly and presented him to the others, adding to Keller, "You see us in better case than last time we met. Dr. Torrens was with you then. He commented unfavorably on the extent of our arsenal. Things have changed remarkably, wouldn't you say? Torrens, of all people, is helping to equip us."

"I can hardly believe it's by his own choice."

"No. By command of the queen," said Florian. "I have a warrant, in her own hand, commissioning me to lead irregular troops in support of her own army. In fact, she's given me the equivalent rank of general." Florian laughed. "But never mind that. We are all civilians here and pay little attention to such things.

"Our work is very simple," he went on. "We get ourselves killed, although we try to do that as little as possible. When the Regians invaded, they expected no resistance. They did not come in great strength. The queen was able to stop them at the Alma when she destroyed the bridge. We're holding them there, keeping them from fording the river—a costly operation for us. But it has allowed Augusta to regroup her own forces, to play for time until the nearby garrisons join her. The Regians, you can be sure, will order in reinforcements. Heaven help us if they manage to cross the Alma. Augusta will have a rather formidable army to face. So shall we. As her front-line troops, we'll bear the brunt of it."

Keller had wanted to speak privately with him, but Florian insisted on first taking him on an inspection tour. Florian swung onto a white mare and he and the journalist, on his own horse, set off through the encampment.

Word of Florian's approach raced ahead. In workaday clothes, red ribbons around their sleeves or red cockades in their hats, Florian's people crowded to cheer him, pressing so closely the horses could scarcely make their way.

Some stretched out their hands, eager to touch his stirrup iron, or the skirt of the old blue greatcoat which had become as famous as its owner.

Once they were alone, Keller told Florian what had happened since their last meeting and why he had come.

"Old Kasperl honors us," Florian said, "but if you're here because you feel some obligation to me, I must, with all thanks, refuse. There is no debt. If you insist there is, then I hereby cancel it.

"No one is here out of obligation," he added, "unless it is out of obligation to what we believe in. Brotherhood, freedom, justice—there's a good chance, my friend, of turning these words into the facts of our lives; indeed, into something the world has never seen before."

"Even under the monarchy?" asked Keller. "Torrens is a good man and a good friend; but he has begun taking steps, with noblest intentions, that may turn the monarchy back into a tyranny. I can't sit by and watch. That's one reason I've come here."

"What happens to the monarchy makes little difference in the long run. It must fall, sooner or later, one way or another. Here and now, we make a new beginning. If you believe that, I welcome you."

"Old Kasperl finds it easier to laugh than to believe," replied Keller. "I appall myself to find that now I wish to believe. Try to, in any case. A deplorable lapse, and one I may come to regret. You say I owe you nothing. Perhaps I owe something to myself."

"I can find some useful place for you on my staff."

"I decline the honor," said Keller. "Old Kasperl may be a public figure, his creator prefers to be a private soldier. It seems more appropriate."

"As you please," Florian said after a few moments, "though I don't relish Old Kasperl putting himself at risk. We can hardly afford to lose him."

"I was as much at risk in the days of the unlamented Cabbarus," Keller said. "That doesn't trouble me, now that my water rats are safe and sound."

Sparrow's rations did not outlast the day. She had given most of them to Weasel. Toward sundown, she began casting about for food and shelter. She sighted a crowd of men and women heading across a field. They were day laborers, tenant farmers, and peasants. Most carried the common tools of their trade: pitchforks and scythes, axes and rakes.

Seeking one war, Sparrow had stumbled into another. To many of the country folk, the enemies were not Regians but local landlords and masters of the great estates. The tenantry, for years, had labored without pay on their master's private roads, had been cheated of even their meager share in the harvests. Their houses had been torn down for lack of a few months' rent; the women had gone begging on the roads while their men poached game on the hunting preserves, to be flogged or hanged if they were caught. The Regian invasion had been a match set to a powder keg.

Sparrow tugged at one man's sleeve and asked where they were going. He gave an answer that meant little to her.

"La Jolie."

"Is there anything to eat there?"

"More than you've seen in your life."

This was all Sparrow needed to hear. Clutching Weasel's hand, she slipped through the crowd, eager to be among the first arrivals. She could hardly believe there would be food enough to go round, and she was determined to have her portion.

They moved past a pair of iron gates that had been broken and were hanging lopsided from their hinges. The crowd quickened its pace, streaming across garden beds and gravel walkways. The house was the biggest that Sparrow had ever seen, except for the Juliana. A number of people were halted before a wide expanse of stone steps. Many held torches. She pushed her way to the front rank.

The house itself was dark, but in the torchlight Sparrow glimpsed the faces of servant women peering from the casements. Half a dozen men stood at the door. One held a light fowling piece. He was shouting at the mob to go away.

"Stand aside, Otho," someone shouted back. "Let us in, you won't be hurt."

The man did not move. Some of the farmers had drifted to the far side of the house. Sparrow heard glass shatter. One of the outbuildings had started blazing. Horses whinnied in the stables. At this, Otho, the man with the fowling piece, seemed uncertain what to do. A couple of the grooms and stableboys with him ran toward the commotion in the rear of the courtyard. The crowd pressed forward. The man pointed his weapon.

A stone flew through the air and smashed one of the

casements. The man suddenly fired. The report was a trivial snapping sound. One of the farm laborers staggered back, cursing and holding his arm. An angry murmur ran through the crowd. As Otho prepared to reload, someone threw a pitchfork at him. The tines struck him full in the chest. He dropped his gun and sat down, staring at the pitchfork and fumbling to pull it out. One of the servants tried to drag him into the house, but gave it up and plunged after his fellows, who had already fled through the door.

Weasel, during his career as a scavenger, had calmly dealt with any number of dead bodies, but never one that had been killed before his eyes. For some reason, he burst out crying. Sparrow gritted her teeth. She wanted food.

Weasel, to make matters worse, had begun throwing up. By the time Sparrow attended to him, the crowd had forced the doors and were inside. Weasel tried to hang back, but she dragged him in after her.

She had no idea where to find the kitchen. The grand hall was filled with people hacking at the paintings on the wall and chopping at the furniture. Some had seized whatever objects they could carry and were running from the house.

Sparrow stumbled on, not daring to let go of Weasel, who was bawling and blubbering. The kitchen, by the time she reached it, had been ransacked. The doors of the larder had been smashed open, most of the contents scattered along with the pots, pans, and utensils. A cook and a scullery maid lay in the midst of it. She knelt and tried to scoop up what eatables remained, urging Weasel to do likewise.

Until then, Sparrow had been undaunted. Now she screamed and turned away. She put her wrist to her mouth and bit down hard. Among the broken victuals lay a hand like a large white spider.

She was terrified of spiders.

# 12

"The Muse is a faithless wench," said Stock. "If she wants no more of me, I want no more of her. Let her go to the devil."

The poet glumly swatted one of the stinging flies that swarmed in the camp as the weather had grown warmer. He took a sheaf of grubby papers from his jacket. "Do you remember, once we talked about knights and paladins? I actually started writing something of that sort, you know. It began splendidly. I was going to show you when I finished. Since I can't finish, I hereby renounce it."

He made as if to tear up the pages. Theo pulled them away. "That's nonsense. I'll keep them for you. Tomorrow, you'll change your mind. You'll be glad to have them back."

"I doubt it." Stock, nevertheless, protested no further when Theo tucked the pages into his own jacket but only added, "My inspiration has fled. I simply don't feel that way anymore. Take those wretched stanzas if you like; just promise you won't read them."

The poet had not said a word about the stolen food since the night the Monkey brought it; nor had Theo. The Monkey had made other forays after that. It had become taken for granted. Theo wondered if Justin knew. He suspected he did.

More questionable, to Theo, was the next harvest. As far as he could see, there would be none. The fields had been neither plowed nor sown. In the outlying farms, the Regians had broken into stores of seed corn. The farmers themselves, in some cases, had destroyed their own grain rather than see it fall into Regian hands.

He spoke about it to Justin, who seemed untroubled. "We'll manage," he told Theo. "Everything will be dealt with. It's not your concern."

Justin's face had lost flesh; the cheekbones jutted sharply, the scar stood out like a piece of rope. "I've planned for whatever happens."

He did not say what those plans were. Theo did not raise the question again and finally put it out of his mind. Autumn was the distant future. Everything was distant except the camp itself, the ground he slept on, and the reek of his own body. The woods had come into full, rich foliage; he was glad of it only because it gave better concealment. As much as he thought of Mickle, and often dreamed of her, she was in a different, remote world. He had no idea what she was doing.

He had to believe she was safe.

He tried not to wonder if she still thought of him.

Luther had not come back. There had been no word from Florian, and few messages from Rina in Eschbach. Lack of information on the Regian troop movements hampered the raids. Often, the marauders were fought off and forced to withdraw, having done little damage, returning empty-handed. Justin hoarded what ammunition remained for his cannon and did not order the gun into action.

Their fortunes, early in July, took a turn for the better. Stock, leading one of the raiding parties, came back exultant. His face was bright with sweat. Even before reporting to Justin, he could not resist crowing to Theo.

"Magnificent! You should have seen us. Not a man lost on our side. Those Regian pigs—we did in the lot of them. Most, anyway. We got half the supply train, too. If I'd had more people, I'd have taken it all." He added, under his breath, "Don't tell Justin, but it was a lucky accident. We just happened to stumble on them."

The poet laughed and clapped his hands. Theo had never seen him so gleeful, even when he had finished a sonnet.

The company celebrated and stuffed themselves. Justin commended Stock before the whole troop. The Monkey watched, grinning happily, nodding at Stock with approval, as if he and the poet had been accomplices.

Next day, the Regians burned one of the villages in reprisal. Theo saw it with his own eyes. Justin, who had not yet allowed Theo on a raiding party, continued to use him as a scout. On that day, Theo had offered to go into the village itself and try to learn what he could.

His offer proved useless. By the time he came within half a mile, he saw the smoke. He pressed on, not understanding at first what had happened. Closer, he halted on a ridge overlooking the valley. Some of the buildings were already aflame. Figures in uniforms were herding the villagers into the open fields; from the distance, they all looked very small. The smell of burning wood and thatch drifted up to the ridge. He watched for a time, then did the only thing possible: He turned around and went back.

"The Regians are fools," Justin said, when Theo reported to him. "The more of this sort of business, the more these country folk will be up in arms. Yes, we can expect some new volunteers."

"What about the rest? The old people, the children?"

"They'll make do," Justin answered. "In any case, they can't help us much."

As Justin foretold, a handful of villagers later made their way to the camp, though not as many as he had hoped. The Regians had hanged several, a few had been shot resisting the soldiers. Justin was disappointed.

Newcomers, by now, outnumbered the original company. At the beginning, Justin had known every one of his troop by name. Now there were too many, and sometimes he was uncertain even of the names of the officers he appointed. He occasionally went through the camp, stopping to talk with some of them. More often he stayed apart and saw only his staff.

Theo feared that Justin's aloofness would dampen the company's spirits. It surprised him when the contrary happened. The newcomers, some of whom had rarely spoken face to face with Justin, talked of him with a kind of awe as they sat around their cook fires.

The Monkey, who had always called Justin "Captain" addressed him now as "Colonel," so glibly and naturally that Justin never noticed the change; or, if he did, he said nothing about it.

Stock had caught a Regian: a young corporal of infantry, rawboned and ruddy-faced, who would have looked more comfortable in a farm laborer's clothing than in his disheveled uniform. Stock had laid hold of him on the spur of the moment. His raiding party had set fire to a supply tent; the man had suddenly appeared. The burly poet had jumped on him and, with the help of his marauders, hauled him away at the end of a rope, making him run to keep up with them. The corporal, despite his ordeal, was only a little more begrimed and breathless than his captor.

"I only took him because I thought he might tell us something," the poet said to Theo. "The fellow's a noncommissioned officer, after all. He has to know what those pigs are up to. Come on, let's see what Justin makes of him."

He hustled his prize to Justin's tent. The Regian, his hands still bound, stood awkwardly. He looked as if he wanted to sit down.

Justin began questioning him sharply about supply trains and ammunition stores. The corporal frowned, a little bemused, and shook his head. Apparently, he could not speak the common language, for he answered in a broad peasant dialect that was barely understandable. Justin, who had caught less than half a dozen phrases, repeated his questions. The man grinned good-naturedly. It was clear he understood Justin no better than Justin understood him, and it seemed to strike him as humorous. The Regian glanced around, smiling and shrugging his shoulders.

"Let me try," said Theo. "Up north, in my province, the peasant accent isn't too much different." He turned to the Regian and, with some difficulty, rephrased what

Justin had asked. At this, the corporal babbled out such a spate of patois that Theo motioned him to go slower.

"It's a new regiment," Theo explained to Justin. "They haven't been here long. They were ordered in a few days ago."

"Good," said Justin. "He'll have seen new supply trains from the Col."

"I asked him. He says not."

"I don't believe him. All right, then. What's his regiment planning to do?"

"He doesn't know that, either," said Theo, after listening closely to the corporal's answer.

"Tell him he's a liar."

The Regian had understood the tone of Justin's reply if not the words, and blurted a hasty protest that also sounded half-apologetic. He seemed eager to please, but did not know how.

Justin struck the man in the face. The soldier stumbled back and lost his balance. The Monkey, who had come into the tent during this, hauled him to his feet. The Regian's nose was bleeding, but he continued to smile as if it had all been an unhappy misunderstanding. Spitting and clearing his throat, he muttered rapidly to Theo.

"I don't think he does know anything," said Theo. "He swears he'd tell you if he did. I believe him."

"I don't," said Justin. "Take him out. Keep at him. He's trying to make fools of us."

"Let me have him," put in the Monkey, as Theo and Stock led the man from the tent. In spite of Theo's protest, the Monkey collared the prisoner and marched him into the woods. Theo would have followed. Stock held him back.

"Let be," said the poet. "It's not up to you now."

"The Monkey won't do better," Theo said angrily. "To the devil with the whole business."

The Monkey came back after a time. He was alone. "You were right," he admitted to Theo. "He didn't know more than what he told you. I'm satisfied of that now. Nothing to be had. I let him go."

"What?" cried Stock. "You fool!"

"Well, then," answered the Monkey, "let's say I released him."

The Monkey hitched up his belt and went off to report to Justin. Stock kicked at a tuft of weeds.

"I'm sorry I brought him in."

"Yes. I am, too."

The poet grimaced. "Damned waste of time."

Stock was killed a week later.

To make up for the useless prisoner, Stock had proposed to capture a better one. With Rosana and a few others, the poet offered to make a foray that night into one of the Regian command posts.

"We'll go at it very fast," said Stock. "Go in, get out in a hurry. This time, we'll try for an officer. Who knows, with luck we might even gobble up a general."

Justin did not approve at first. The poet, caught up in his own enthusiasm, insisted. He reminded Justin how badly they needed information. In the end, Justin agreed.

"If you botch it, though," he warned, "you'll answer to me. Lose any of your people, I'll court-martial you."

Justin laughed then, but Theo could not be certain whether or not he was in earnest.

Theo urged Stock to take him along. The poet refused. "It's not that I don't want to," Stock assured him. "But Rosana and the others—we're used to each other, you see." He grinned. "I mean to do something even the Monkey couldn't pull off."

The party set off at nightfall, expecting to be back within a day. Two days passed without a sign of them. This in itself was not unusual; some of the parties had stayed out longer. But later one of the outposts reported firing from the bottomlands below the camp.

Theo had never seen Justin so agitated. Until then, Theo had imagined that Justin cared more for the cannon than for any individual. It was not altogether true. Justin was fonder of the poet than Theo had supposed.

Though it was broad daylight, Justin ordered the Monkey to form a party and set off immediately. Justin himself led them. Given no orders one way or the other, Theo rode with them. Justin did not seem to notice he was there.

The Monkey, who had gone some way ahead, turned his mount. He whistled through his teeth and beckoned to Justin. They rode into a clearing. The Monkey had already dismounted.

Theo jumped down from his mare. What looked like a side of beef had been propped against a tree trunk. The eyes were open, staring at him. The mouth seemed full of red mud. It took him several moments to realize it was Stock.

Theo grew aware of the Monkey cursing endlessly and monotonously. He paid no attention. Something should be done about Stock's body; this seemed a matter of great importance. He stood for what he felt was a long time, considering what would be best. Rosana and the others in Stock's party lay awkwardly about the turf. Like the poet, they had been stripped and badly cut up. The Monkey was giving some kind of instructions about burying them.

Justin had come beside him. His face was white, the scar working and twitching. He was talking, as far as Theo could understand, about animals.

It was, Theo found, an odd topic. He finally grasped that Justin meant Regians. They should, Justin was saying, be punished for all this. Theo agreed. He offered to do it.

Justin said Theo had no stomach for what was necessary. He also suggested that Theo was a coward, and had shown this at Nierkeeping. Theo, a little hurt, assured him it was not the case. He offered to prove it. He explained his thought to Justin. He wanted the Monkey and some others to go with him. They would find who had done it. To Theo, it seemed that he and Justin were discussing the question calmly, in an intense but reasonable conversation.

They were, in fact, screaming at each other.

Justin, at last, told him he could have the Monkey, half a dozen of the newcomers, but no more than four of the seasoned troopers.

"I don't want prisoners taken," Justin said. "Not this time."

"No," said Theo. "No prisoners."

It was, Theo considered, generous of Justin, and he thanked him. His desire had become very narrow and simple: to kill everyone wearing a Regian uniform; failing that, as many as possible. It seemed a modest and sensible goal.

He was not sane enough to realize he had gone somewhat mad; he had only gone mad enough to believe himself completely sane.

# PART III
# THE KESTREL

# 13

King Constantine was playing with tin soldiers in a sandbox. The small, beautifully crafted figures represented his own units of cavalry, foot, and artillery; another set, the Westmark detachments, to the extent that General Erzcour and the Regian staff had been able to determine them. Constantine also had two special and slightly taller figures: himself and Queen Augusta.

The sandbox, as large as the war map set up on one side of the tent, had been sculpted to show a miniature Westmark. Little artificial forests spread over the contoured hills, the rivers had been painted bright blue. It was a lovely piece of workmanship. Constantine had already decided he would keep it permanently somewhere after the war ended.

His Majesty had chosen to wear the uniform of a lieutenant of hussars, without decorations. The notion of dressing like a serving officer of minor rank amused him. This morning, however, the king had shed his tunic, belt, and saber. It was too warm for such trappings.

Duke Conrad fanned himself with a handkerchief.

Unlike his nephew, he observed the proprieties of royal costume. He continued, in spite of the heat, to wear the white-and-gold tunic that custom prescribed for royalty in the field. He sighed and mopped his forehead.

"Do leave off, Connie," he said to his nephew. "You've been at it all morning. It gets on my nerves. It is a useless exercise."

"Yes, it certainly is," replied the king. He had been contemplating moving some of his miniature brigades closer to the Alma, but changed his mind and left them in position. "No substitute for the real thing. I don't see why you won't let me visit the front. You said you would."

"I said you should move your headquarters into Mull," Conrad answered. "I still say so. There, at least, we should be decently housed. I cannot understand why you insist on living in a tent, like some sort of Trebizonian nomad."

"It's a fine tent," said Constantine. The royal pavilion was, indeed, an elaborate structure. Of heavy canvas, with interior partitions, it had as many chambers and antechambers as a suite of apartments. Constantine's sleeping quarters and those of his uncle were at the rear; the sandbox had been set on a table in the spacious front area, which was furnished with field desks and folding chairs. "We're soldiers in battle, aren't we? I want to get used to the hardships of campaigning. So, we must rough it in good spirit."

"Tents stink," said the duke. "It is their nature to stink. All the more at this time of year."

"At this time of year," Constantine repeated wickedly. "I didn't count on spending the summer here."

The king's remark was pointed not so much at his uncle as at General Erzcour, who was bent over a stack of reports at one of the field desks. The comment and its barb did not go unnoticed. Erzcour stopped his work and approached the king at the sandbox.

"Allow me to explain, Your Majesty," said Erzcour, "that actual combat is the least part of any war. Time is the great factor, whereas the engagement of troops—"

"Armies don't fight, then? I'd have thought otherwise," broke in the king. "Unless you mean the Regian army."

Erzcour reddened. He had changed his former uniform for that of a Regian field commander, and it had been ill tailored. It chafed him under the arms, and he was in no mood to be twitted by a boy, king or otherwise. Nevertheless, he kept a grip on his temper. Erzcour had given up any pretense of maintaining his rank in the army of Westmark. He was now officially a member of the Regian general staff, continually under the eye of Duke Conrad. To squabble openly with the king would make an unpleasant situation unbearable. He decided to play schoolmaster.

"A battle, Your Majesty, is merely the culmination, the climax of careful preparation, of thorough staff work. The dull business of operational orders, transport, baggage, rations. All this must be well in hand before so much as a shot is fired. The first rule of warfare, Majesty, is: Do not fight a battle until you are able to win it."

"When do we do that?" demanded Constantine. "Damn it, Erzcour, we're bloody well not winning anything at all."

Along with his moustache, the king had been cultivating a soldierly manner of speaking. Neither one had provided him with satisfaction; both, despite his nurturing, had remained pale and thin.

He reached into the sandbox and picked up the figure of Augusta, looking at it with frank admiration. "Beggar Queen, if you like; but I think she's a smashing good general. She's in personal command, isn't she? Yes, as I wanted to be and shouldn't have let you talk me out of it. If things keep on as they are, I will take command. I'm king, after all." He grinned. "Too bad that Augusta didn't leave things to her own generals."

"I, too," said Conrad, "should appreciate knowing why we have won nothing."

The duke felt testy. The heat was stifling and the flies were abominable during the day; at night he shivered on an uncomfortable camp bed. During such sleepless hours, he gave considerable thought to Constantine. It was an enormous temptation to let his nephew have his way and inspect the Alma front; one of those night thoughts he preferred not to bring into daylight.

He was glad, meantime, for the occasion to turn his annoyance from Constantine to Erzcour. "According to our plans—that is to say, your plans—this affair should have been over in a matter of weeks. Perhaps, General, your strategy contained some little flaw?"

"Your Highness," replied Erzcour, stiffening, "my strategy was perfect."

"Then we must reproach our enemy for not obediently doing their part correctly? Or did they not find it so perfect?"

"There are unforeseen events in every war," said

Erzcour. "I confess, Your Highness, I was more shocked and dismayed than yourself at the conduct of the Westmark regiments. Their refusal to obey direct orders of their superiors was a reprehensible breach of discipline. Such gross insubordination is shameful. It is a violation of their sacred oath as soldiers.

"Furthermore, the entry of irregular units is deplorable. This Florian is no better than a criminal. That Queen Augusta should have any dealings with him I find frankly detestable. I have only contempt for such an action on her part. They are common cutthroats, bandits. One gang of them in the Domitians recently set upon one of our infantry companies. You have no doubt seen the report. The atrocities practiced on them—" Erzcour shook his head. "Not war, Your Highness, butchery. I promise you they shall be repaid in kind."

Erzcour went on, "As for the campaign in its broader aspects, it is progressing well. There have been no strategic miscalculations, only tactical misadventures. The art of the soldier is to accept them and turn them to his advantage."

"Misadventures are expensive," said Conrad. "These bandits, as you call them, not only strike at our supply lines. They might as well have their fingers in our treasury. Worse than cutting our throats, they're costing us money. The minister of finance is not pleased as the minister of war demands larger funds. We should, I think, give all those fellows commissions in our own regiments. It would be cheaper to pay them than to fight them."

Despite his sore temper, Duke Conrad could not help

laughing at his own witticism. General Erzcour found it less humorous.

"War," he replied, "is not an occupation for paupers."

"Indeed it is not," said Conrad, "nor does Regia have intention of becoming one. I keep a close eye on military expenditures and recommend you do the same."

Talk of money bored Constantine. He put back the figure of Queen Augusta. "Shall we have some lemonade?"

"Yes, Connie. Let us, for heaven's sake, have lemonade." The duke's uniform was damp with sweat, thanks to his nephew and his general. "And some sherbet."

He called an orderly. At the same time, one of the aides came to report that Baron Montmollin had ridden into camp and awaited His Majesty's pleasure.

"Send him in," said Conrad. "He's the only intelligent man in this whole dismal business. He had sense enough to take a house in Mull."

"He's not a soldier," said Constantine.

"He should be glad of that," said the duke.

Montmollin did not appear to have profited from whatever comfort he enjoyed in Mull. He was as elegantly dressed as ever, and barbered as well as could be expected in the provinces. His gray eyes, however, had gone deeper into their sockets, and the aristocrat's face was an unhealthy color.

"Ah. Here is Montmollin come to cheer us up," said Conrad. "We are having lemonade. Will you join us? General Erzcour was about to tell us how to win the war. I hope, at least, he was."

"Forgive me for interrupting him," said Montmollin. He and Erzcour no longer spoke directly to each other. Montmollin had been firmly against the general's decision to join the Regian staff; on this, there had been hard words between them.

"It can be done quite simply," said Erzcour. "Your Highness expressed concern over military expenditures. We have an old saying in Westmark: Do not spoil the ship for a pennyworth of tar."

"Yes, but we have already spent a great number of pennies," replied Conrad, "and have had very little tar for our money."

"We are at an extremely critical moment," said Erzcour. "Our forces will soon establish themselves firmly on the west bank of the Alma. That I promise. It is inevitable. They must, however, be strongly reinforced."

"What, you ask for more men?" returned Conrad. "When we began, you assured me only a few regiments would suffice."

"So it seemed at the time," said Erzcour. "Now, nothing less than total commitment is required. Our units must be brought up to full strength. They must fight with the greatest severity against the enemy, and apply the strictest possible measures to the civilian population. Also, we must support our troops with increased supplies. The cost will be high, but only in the short run. As we shall thus end the war faster, in the long run it will be cheaper.

"Given Regia's complete military resources," continued Erzcour, "I shall be able to apply a new strategy, one that cannot fail."

"I should like to know your new strategy before I pay for it," said Conrad. "We have a saying: Never buy a pig in a poke."

Erzcour glanced at the baron. "I shall explain it in detail at our military council."

"War is not for civilians, eh?" said Conrad, a little more cheerful now that the orderly had carried in a refreshment tray. "Good. I agree with you in principle. We shall not hold back. I favor anything that will move us forward. I should, indeed, be glad for anything that would move us out of this tent." He turned to Montmollin. "Dear Baron, can you not use all your charm and persuasion upon Connie? Convince him, Baron, to leave this canvas hotbed."

"Your Highness," said Montmollin, "I have come for that express purpose."

"Bravo!" cried the duke. "High time. You listen to him, Connie."

"More than leaving your tent, Majesty," said Montmollin, "I urge you to leave Westmark altogether."

Constantine blinked at him. Duke Conrad chuckled and raised his glass. "The baron has a delicious wit. He is about to pronounce, surely, one of his epigrams. We are waiting eagerly."

Until now, Baron Montmollin had been able to sum up most of his opinions in a well-turned line. Of late, this gift had left him. He regretted the loss. It had kept the truth at a polite distance and made it more graceful.

The baron found nothing graceful in what he was compelled now to say: "We began our endeavors in order to save Westmark, not destroy it. The contrary is happening, and it will worsen if General Erzcour is allowed to continue. The damage that has already taken place, the loss of life—these have gone far beyond our intentions. The war must end here and now, or we shall have no kingdom at all."

The smile had frozen on Conrad's face. "That is your fault, not ours. You assured us it would be a simple, easy matter. We kept our part of the bargain, did we not? You did not keep yours. Now you seriously ask us to withdraw? To have spent a fortune for no gain? My dear Baron—"

"Keep as much of the country as you have already occupied," said Montmollin. "Even that would be better than devastating the rest of it."

"How generous you are," said Conrad. "Yes, we shall most certainly keep that."

"As for the cost," said Montmollin, "to whatever degree it may compensate, I am willing to offer the value of all my personal holdings and resources. They are not inconsiderable."

Conrad leaned forward. "I doubt very much, at this point, that you have any fortune to offer. That you even have a roof over your head. One of our very reliable agents has reported that your estate—La Jolie, is it not?—has been burned. You cannot be unaware of that. You, naturally, have others. Whatever else may happen to them, they will surely not be available to you.

"There have been certain new developments," Conrad went on. "I had not intended going into them now. Since you raise the question, however, this is as good a moment as any.

"I think, Baron, you made an error in refusing Cabbarus a place on your council. He has, in consequence, devoted his services entirely to our interests. Connie and I met with him not long ago. He reminded us of a simple fact we had almost overlooked.

"My dear Baron, do you not understand? Sooner or later, we would have invaded Westmark in any case. Your plan suited our convenience. It might even have been acceptable had it worked as you promised. Since it did not, we continue on our own. It is our war, not yours. Prior agreements no longer apply. Your participation in any ruling council, of course, is also out of the question."

Baron Montmollin had a quick intelligence, but it took him several moments to absorb a sensation he had never experienced: betrayal.

"We are not ungrateful," Conrad was saying. "We shall release you as a hostage—which, indeed, you never were. The best we can offer, however, is safe conduct through our lines. Very little, true. On the other hand, you gave us very little in exchange. Go home, Baron. Wherever that may be."

Montmollin put down his glass. The lemonade had been too cold, it had chilled him. His hands and feet had gone icy and he felt unwell. He turned to King Constantine. It required an effort for him to speak calmly.

"Does Your Majesty approve of this? Have you given your consent to what is nothing short of dishonoring our cause, of breach of faith—"

"Oh, yes," said Constantine. "I think it's only good sense. Don't you, really? Looking at it from our side? Cabbarus is a disgusting creature, but his advice is very sound. I'm sorry, Montmollin, but we have to do what's best for ourselves, don't we?"

"Men of honor," said Montmollin, "Keep their word."
Constantine grinned at him. "Kings don't."

# 14

"There's a hawk." Justin pointed beyond the ridge. High above, against the cloudless blue, the bird seemed to hang motionless.

"It's a windhover," said Theo. "Kestrel, we call it in Dorning, where I come from." It was the first one he had seen here. "It's hunting. They're small but very quick. They scream before they kill."

Justin laughed. "Vicious little creatures."

"I think not. Animals aren't vicious. They only do what they do."

He and Justin had ridden ahead to pick a new campsite. For two weeks, they had been continually moving. Justin was anxious to get well out of the area. Since Theo's attack on one of the Regian companies, several punitive forces had been sent up. So far, Justin had avoided them.

Theo reined in beside him, waiting. Justin had wanted to talk privately. The mare snuffled and tossed her head. Theo watched the kestrel for a time as it soared on the wind currents. In the higher reaches of the Domitians, the foliage had already begun a subtle change of color. Summer would be short.

"He was a genius, you know," Justin said abruptly. It was as if he had been holding a long conversation with himself and had spoken the end of it aloud.

It startled Theo. It was the first time Justin had mentioned Stock. Theo had even begun to wonder if Justin ever thought of him. Florian, he remembered, said that things dropped into Justin's mind and disappeared. Then he realized he himself had not been able to talk about Stock's death.

"The laureate of our cause," Justin said. "A great poet."

"No." Theo had lost sight of the kestrel as it tacked and sailed below the ridge. It had no doubt found something. "No. He wasn't a great poet. He was a good poet. He might have been better. That's the real loss, don't you see?"

"He was our laureate of freedom," Justin insisted.

When Theo had come back from the raid, he and Justin had gone through Stock's belongings. There was nothing worth sharing out among the company. To the sheaf of works in various stages of completion, Theo was about to add Stock's abandoned poem. Justin wanted to read it, which he did. Although Theo told him Stock's own opinion, Justin thought highly of it and kept it aside for himself. The others, Theo tied up and packed in his saddlebag.

While doing so, he suddenly noticed his hands. The reddish crust under his torn fingernails puzzled him. His boots had been blood-spattered; his breeches had been soaked and were already dry and stiffening. He could not imagine how anything had gotten under his nails.

"You avenged a comrade," Justin was saying. "You've done well. That's what I wanted to talk to you about. I can tell you now, I had my doubts. I wasn't really sure you could. I'm glad to admit I was wrong. A good officer isn't afraid to do that, you know. Yes, and along those lines: the question of my second-in-command."

Justin gave him his frank, boyish look. "You mustn't mind if I tell you—I want to be clear on all this—I appointed the Monkey."

"Good. The best choice."

"Yes," Justin said. "But he didn't want it. He really didn't. I tried to convince him. He said it didn't suit him. I suppose he'd rather not have the responsibility. I understand that. What I mean is, he was my first choice. I won't hide that from you. Now I'll ask: Will you be my second?"

"I don't care one way or the other. If that's what you want, yes."

"Marvelous," said Justin. "It's settled." He took up the reins. "Do you remember?" he added. "That day at the mill, when Stock chose our names? I liked that. You, I think, shall be—well, why not Kestrel?"

"As good as any." He remembered feeling left out when Stock had chosen none for him. Now it made no difference.

"I must get word to Florian," Justin said. "I'll report what happened and that you've taken Stock's post."

"No. I don't want Florian to know that. Kestrel, nothing more. No need for him to know who it is."

Justin shrugged. "As you please. Yes, I agree it would be better that way."

A few weeks later, because of their growing number, Justin divided the company in two. The larger detachment he led himself. The rest was Theo's command. The Monkey, surprisingly, gravitated to Theo. He showed no sign of resentment at Theo's new rank. If anything, he looked on Theo with the pride and admiration of a teacher for a favorite student. He even addressed Theo as Colonel, accepting him as being on equal footing with Justin. The Monkey was an eager, invaluable helper. Theo could not have done as well without him.

It was the Monkey, Theo chose to believe, who had started the terrifying screaming during the first raid after Theo's promotion. Before dawn, approaching the Regian outpost, the men had been silent, walking their horses, taking pains to keep their harnesses from jingling. There was barely the creak of saddles. The sabers had been oiled so as not to scrape when drawn. Theo had ordered firearms to be used only as a last resort.

Going into the attack, someone began a high-pitched keening, not unlike a kestrel's. It spread, growing louder until they were all doing it: an endless shriek, rising as if from a single throat. Theo glimpsed the Monkey, teeth bared, head flung back. At the time, he assumed it was the Monkey who had started the war cry. Later, he could not trust his recollection. It might have been anyone, even himself.

From then on, they made a practice of it. No one ordered it; it seemed the most natural thing to do.

The early part of autumn continued bright and cool. Then, for a time, the weather broke and there were days of driving rain. For Theo, there were no days at all, only periods of light and darkness. They might have been years for all he knew or cared. Time had no meaning for him, it had neither beginning nor end. He was simply there, going about his work.

Against the sharp mountain wind, the men layered themselves with as much clothing as they could salvage. Some had stocking caps, others simply wrapped cloths around their heads. Someone—probably the Monkey—had given Theo a vest crudely cut from a sheepskin. The fleece, untreated, smelled rank. He did not notice it.

During late autumn, the company increased its number; not only with men from the nearby villages and farms, but still more from considerable distances. They brought with them accounts of burned houses, hangings, shootings. To Theo, these had become commonplace. He barely listened to them. The men's faces were all alike to him, as dirty and stubble-bearded as his own. Some, he realized, were younger than the others; to him, they looked like children. He vaguely recalled he had been a child in Dorning, but the memory carried no weight. He was what he was now, and a stranger in his own past.

He was Colonel Kestrel and had never been anything else. As the newcomers arrived, many asked for him by that name. Justin did not appear at all envious. He seemed, on the contrary, to enjoy Kestrel's growing reputation. The more ferocious Kestrel's raids, the more they attracted new volunteers. Those who joined now were different from the ones of earlier days: more desperate, more enraged; men already with a Regian price on their heads; homeless, without family, and with nothing left to lose. Kestrel suited them.

"What we'll be able to do, eh?" one of them said to Theo. "After this is over, no matter how it comes out, there'll be enough of us to make them all take notice. Someday, then"—he slashed the edge of his hand across his throat—"no more aristocrats, nor kings; nor queens either, for that matter."

Theo did not answer him. He had just heard from another newcomer that in some villages the women were now in the habit of whispering to their fretful children: "Hush, hush! Or the big Kestrel will come eat you."

Suddenly, to his surprise, he thought of something he had told Florian at the mill. They had been talking about Jacobus. The old scholar had written that people were gentle by nature, and Florian asked if Theo believed that. Theo had answered that he did. It was, he told Florian, the way he felt, and he was no different from anyone else.

He wondered if he had told the truth then.

He was afraid that he had.

As autumn ended, Regian detachments forced a crossing of the Alma. The queen had retreated from Carlsbruch. By the time Theo learned this, it was old news.

It had already happened, there was nothing he could have done about it.

# 15

Colonel Witz and Count Las Bombas were in torment: Witz, because he itched for a battle, yearned to fling himself and his regiments against the advancing hordes in one grand, heroic charge. Las Bombas had indigestion.

Mickle decided to deal first with the more difficult. The count, hunched over a bench in the farmhouse she had taken for her newest headquarters, was complaining as usual about the porridge.

"It's the army breakfast," she reminded him, "and none of us, including my military adviser, will eat anything different. We agreed on that. It's not so bad, you know. It's better than the oatmeal they fed us when I was in the Home for Repentant Girls."

"Lumps," grumbled the count. "More lumps than porridge." He continued, nevertheless, to spoon it down until he emptied the bowl. He turned his attention to the biscuit, rapping it loudly on the bench. "Witz, you've mixed ammunition with the rations. These things are fatal."

"Keep chewing," advised Musket, squatting by the fireplace. He had kept the saber commandeered at the Alma and had since acquired a brace of pistols. Armed to the teeth, he had so far used none of these weapons but was eager to do so; he sided, therefore, with the impetuous Witz. "You haven't lost any weight."

"Wind, my boy," said Las Bombas. "Nothing but wind."

Leaving the count and Musket to their discussion, Mickle took up the question of Witz. After Alma, the devoted Witz had taken on himself the instruction of his beloved sovereign. He had explained military organization and procedures, the deployment of troops, the use of terrain, and the eternal paperwork. She had absorbed it all, even more quickly than Torrens himself could have expected.

Then she leaped beyond her teacher. Along with her gifts of mimicry and ventriloquism, she discovered another. A map, once studied, stayed in her mind. She could summon it up whenever she chose. She told the astonished Witz that it was only a mental trick, but it merely increased his admiration for his commander.

What she foresaw would happen had happened. The Regians had forded the Alma in strength, despite every effort of Florian's people. With his irregulars as rear guard, she had ordered a general retreat. Cold judgment told her that any other course would have brought sure disaster.

The Regians wanted a pitched battle. She would not give it. She had fallen back from Carlsbruch, refusing to let her troops be shattered by Regian artillery, and regrouped at Altus-Birkenfeld—Las Bombas observing that the name was bigger than the hamlet. By retreating, she had lost few supplies and saved her army. She hoarded lives like a miser.

Witz, however, despite his continuous calculations, had thrown caution to the wind. He was in agony at the constant retreating, though he knew it was militarily sound. He wanted a battle, with himself leading the charge. He believed it could be won.

"Beg to report," said Witz, "your troops, including myself, are prepared to do or die."

"I'd rather you just do," said Mickle. "The point is to have as little dying as possible. You, Colonel, I can hardly spare."

Witz blushed, as he always did when his sovereign addressed him so directly. He trotted after Mickle, who had gone to the map table. He had still not lost hope for a glorious sacrifice.

"We're not going to fight them here," Mickle said. "Let them come on. The farther they advance, the longer they stretch their supply lines. We retreat and shorten ours. If they attack and we withdraw, we leave them punching away at an empty sack. They bombarded Carlsbruch—but we weren't there. They wasted ammunition. We saved ours."

Las Bombas, still grinding on the biscuit, joined them. "Excellent strategy. As an old campaigner, I'd be the first to recommend meeting them head on, if I thought we'd get anything from it. At the moment, Florian's other people up in the Domitians are doing our work for us. From all reports, they're playing the very devil with our uninvited guests. There's a new commander, too. Colonel Kestrel or some such; a real madman, a bloodthirsty fellow, very good at his trade."

"Luther told me Theo was going to the Domitians." Mickle stopped short. She had tried to keep her personal fears and feelings on one side of a barrier and the war on another. The barrier often broke down.

"Don't worry," said Las Bombas. "He'll manage. He's a lad of sense and caution: good qualities, at least in these circumstances."

Mickle turned again to the map, though she knew it by heart. She had, these past days, made her own private calculations. She wondered if Witz, despite his eager gallantry, had already done the same and if he had come to the same answer. Las Bombas, she thought, was shrewd enough to see it without need of arithmetic. Perhaps they both knew and dared not admit it to themselves. Before the rest of her staff came, she decided to speak her mind to the two closest to her.

"There's no way that I can see," she began, glancing from Witz to the count, "there's no way we can do it. We can't win."

Witz looked stunned. Forgetting all forms of address and courtesy even toward his queen, he burst into a storm of protest. Mickle raised her hand.

"We can't win," she repeated. "Not as things stand. We can hold them off, yes. We can stop them, but we're not strong enough to drive them out of the kingdom."

Witz had fallen silent, chewing miserably on his moustache. Cold rain had begun pattering against the windows. It mixed with the distant rattle of musketry. Florian's skirmishers were busy. He would demand a reckoning, Mickle knew very well. He had told her as much. There were times when she would gladly have turned over the whole command to him, and the throne into the bargain. Nevertheless, she went on as cheerfully as she could.

"That's one thing. There's another. If we can't win, neither can the Regians.

"The days are drawing in," Mickle continued. "Winter's coming. We'll be frozen in our tracks, both sides. Then, next spring we'll all start again, and still be no better off. I don't see how we can turn the tide against them, and at the moment, I don't see how they can turn the tide against us. Meantime, the country is ruined. It's bad enough now. It can only get worse."

"I can't disagree," said Las Bombas, "but I don't know what we can do."

"I do," said Mickle. "I'm going to end it."

"Surrender?" cried Witz, anguished. "Majesty—that's out of the question! No, no, we can't—"

"I didn't say I was going to surrender," Mickle answered. "I said I'm going to end it. I'm going to offer peace terms."

"Majesty, that's the same thing."

"No, it isn't. I won't give them an inch of Westmark. Why should they want it in the first place? If they stop and think, they'll see it will be a hornet's nest for them, with all the countryside against them. They'd never be able to keep order. They should be glad to get shut of it.

"But—I'm willing to give them something better: an open border, so that anyone on either side can come and go freely."

"A fair offer," said Las Bombas. "Hardly enough, though. They won't settle for it."

"There's more. The Regian ports are small and

cramped. They don't have a good one. They've been using ours for years, and paying heavy anchorage fees. Well, now they can use it free. I have some other ideas about trade and lowering custom tolls, but I'll save them and have something to dicker about."

"Now, that's a good bargain," said the count, "and I know one when I see it. By heaven, you might be on to something."

"Majesty," pleaded Witz, "you can't give up all that. Think of the honor of the kingdom."

"Honorable wreckage," said Mickle. "What I'm giving is only fair. The fact is, I was going to do it anyway, as it should have been done long before. Of course," she added, "they don't have to know that. What matters is: The terms are splendid. They'd be fools to refuse."

"There's where the trouble comes in," said Las Bombas. "By the time the generals, the statesmen, and every piddling courtier start picking at them—"

"I know all about that in the Juliana," said Mickle. "That's why I won't have anything to do with them. I'm going to make the offer to King Constantine himself."

The count snorted. "Constantine! He's only a boy, hardly more than a child."

"Yes," Mickle said. "That's why I expect he'll have better sense than his generals and ministers. I'm going to talk with him face to face."

"No chance of that," said Las Bombas. "According to all reports, his headquarters are near Mull. You won't persuade him to come here."

"I don't intend to. I'm going there."

"Not much chance of that, either," said Las Bombas. "You'll have to start with a flag of truce, then a formal meeting with the commanding general, then his superior, and so on. Not to mention Duke Conrad and a few dozen councillors. That's assuming all goes well. The whole business could fall apart before it begins."

"I know that, too," said Mickle. "I won't have any business with them. I'll pass up the lot and go straight to Mull. Constantine will see me, that I promise."

"Dear girl," said Las Bombas, "have you lost your mind? Not possible! The valley's crawling with Regians, as we have good cause to know."

"Exactly why they won't notice me," said Mickle. "I'll be wearing a Regian uniform."

She turned to Musket. "I'll count on you and some of your friends to get one. How you go about doing it I leave to you."

Colonel Witz, listening dumbstruck, at last found his voice. "But—Your Majesty, forgive me, I must protest in strongest possible terms. For you to attempt this alone is, permit me to say, absolutely foolhardy."

"You're right," said Mickle. "While Musket's getting a uniform for me, he'll get another for Count Las Bombas."

The count sat down on the bench. "My dear girl, this is not only lunacy, it's worth our necks. I was a fool to take you out of Marianstat. I'd be a fool twice over to let you try such a scheme. You'd never pull it off."

"With you I would," said Mickle. "You can bamboozle anyone. You'll have no trouble as a Regian officer. We'll be safer than we are here. You'll forge some sort of documents and passes for us. Special emissaries or whatever. From what I've seen of military paperwork, the more confusing the better. We'll get through. I have every confidence in you."

"I can't say the same," replied Las Bombas. "No. This time I won't do it."

"Your Majesty," put in Witz, "even if you reached the king, there is nothing to stop him from seizing you as a prisoner. Or, forgive me for suggesting it, executing you."

"Not likely," said Mickle. "Between monarchs, after all, there has to be some kind of professional courtesy. Very well, I admit there's a risk. My soldiers take risks every day."

"Majesty," said Witz, "allow me to go in your place, as your special envoy."

"It just wouldn't be the same. No, Colonel, it's my errand and I'll do it myself."

"Then," said Witz, "beg to request permission: I shall go with you."

"I can't spare you. I need you here in command. You're to hold your position, if it's at all possible. Fall back if you must. Under no circumstances are you to give battle or do anything foolhardy." She smiled at him. "Leave that to me."

"This is highly irregular," Witz declared. "Military regulations say nothing about a monarch disguised as an enemy soldier; but they certainly forbid a colonel to command an army."

"I almost forgot," said Mickle. "You've been made a general. Congratulations."

She kissed him soundly on both cheeks. Witz turned crimson. While he continued sputtering protests, Mickle called out to Musket, "You, Thumbling, get a move on. I need that uniform."

Las Bombas took the dwarf by the arm. "While you're at it"—he sighed miserably—"you might as well get one for me. Try to find one that fits."

Musket disappeared for the rest of the day and all that night. Next morning, he was back again, proudly displaying two Regian uniforms. Mickle did not ask how he got them and the dwarf volunteered no answers, remarking only that there were now a pair of naked and chilly Regians in the enemy lines.

Las Bombas was dissatisfied. He had resigned himself to Mickle's plan, but found his costume unacceptable. "You might have gotten something larger in the waist," he complained to the dwarf, "and not so wide in the shoulders."

"Make do," retorted Musket. "I'm your coachman, not your tailor."

"Impudence," muttered the count. "It's the war. There's no respect for anything."

Mickle had dressed herself as a Regian sub-lieutenant. She had removed her royal signet ring and hung it around her neck under her tunic. "This will do nicely," she told the count. "I'll be your aide, and you'll do all the talking until we get to Mull."

"Blast that Musket," grumbled the count. "He's made me only a captain. He could have been thoughtful enough to rob a major."

To make up for it, Las Bombas rummaged through his chests and pinned on an assortment of medals and ribbons. He had, meantime, put the final touches on an array of false documents.

"With those papers and all your decorations," Mickle said, "I shouldn't wonder if they gave us a guard of honor the whole way to Mull."

"Yes"—the count sighed—"and straight up against the nearest wall."

The rain had stopped; a cold mist had settled over the countryside. Mickle was grateful. It would give better cover for their departure. Witz had insisted on riding with them almost to the Regian advanced positions. He had arranged for some of the Old Guard, with Musket's help, to cause a diversion allowing the queen and the count to slip through the lines unobserved.

"Permit me to say, Your Majesty—" Witz began, blushing and stammering so much that he was obliged to break off.

"Consider it said," Mickle told him. "You'll hear from us."

Las Bombas had started. Mickle galloped after him.

In a last backward glance before dashing to safety among her enemies, she glimpsed Witz reluctantly turning his mount, the most woebegone general she had ever seen.

Over the following days, they made good progress. The count's medals and documents, and his high-handed military manner, passed them unquestioned from one headquarters to the next. Las Bombas, on the strength of his credentials, commandeered fresh horses and drew officer's rations. He cheered up slightly and had even begun to imagine that Mickle's plan might succeed.

It was only at Eschbach, where they arrived late one evening, that they met with difficulties. Despite the hour, the town teemed with marching troops and more than the ordinary traffic of supply carts. At a barrier across the road, a heavily armed guard halted them. Holding up a lantern, he studied their papers closely, then called for the duty officer.

Las Bombas had broken into a sweat. Mickle's heart was in her mouth. The count, she feared, had made some error in their passes. The officer, on the contrary, was impressed, far more than Mickle wished. He came to rigid attention and saluted sharply but, to her dismay, did not allow them to pass.

"The general must not miss the opportunity of meeting such a distinguished fellow officer," he told Las Bombas. "You, of course, will want to pay your respects."

"Naturally," said the count. "Nothing we should like better. Some other time. Our mission is of the utmost diplomatic delicacy."

"All the more reason, sir," the officer replied. "The general will be eager to hear of it and discuss it with you."

Las Bombas looked ready to collapse. He tried nevertheless to put on as bold a face as he could. "Out of the question. Let us by, sir. We have no time for conversation with General—ah, whoever he is."

The officer looked at him in surprise. "Sir, have you not been advised of it? Eschbach is now headquarters of the supreme commander himself: General Erzcour."

# 16

The officer insisted so strongly, summoning an escort to conduct them to staff headquarters in the town hall, that Las Bombas feared an outright refusal would draw dangerous attention.

"You've never met Erzcour? He's never seen you?" he muttered under his breath as they walked their horses through the crowded street. "No? Good. There's still a chance, then. Don't talk if you can help it. You're only an aide, a lowly sub-lieutenant, not worth a general's glance."

The supreme commander, to the count's intense relief, was in no hurry to receive his visitors. At the town hall, an adjutant reported that General Erzcour sent his regrets at being unable to see them until breakfast next morning. The count and Mickle were taken to their billets on an upper floor of the building, which served as both offices and sleeping quarters.

Left by themselves in a suite of lightly but comfortably furnished chambers, with beds and pillows instead of army cots, the count's military bearing sagged; he paced back and forth, too agitated to appreciate small luxuries.

"Damnable traitor! As if it weren't enough to be delayed here. Erzcour, of all people!"

"There's time," said Mickle. "We have between now and morning to get out. It could be worse."

"It could always be worse," groaned the count, "and usually is. Dear girl, I warned you this would come to no good."

An orderly soon carried in a tray of food with the compliments of the supreme commander. The count, appetite undiminished despite all, attacked the dishes as if they were Erzcour himself.

"Traitor he is," said Las Bombas, "but he puts out a reasonably good dinner. Turncoat! I hope the day comes when he'll be brought to book. Meantime, I'll eat his food out of sheer revenge."

Mickle had gone to the window. As best she could judge, the number of wagons and troops had decreased. A detachment had apparently passed through town. She stood, continuing to watch for a time. Something puzzled her. She could not define it. It was troublesome.

The count's refreshment had brought back some of his confidence. "I'm not sure we should try to leave. We'll be missed, that's bound to raise questions. It might be wiser if I, at least, saw Erzcour. It could be too risky for you to face him unless you must. I'll tell him you're down with a bad case of camp fever or some such. Erzcour has too much on his hands to bother long with visiting officers. The worst might be a few minutes of boring conversation." The count brightened a little as he went on, "In fact, I might even try talking him into giving us an armed escort to Mull."

"If anyone can do it, you can," said Mickle. "I don't know. There's something I have to think about."

"Think about what happens once we're clear of this place. That's the main idea."

Mickle still felt uneasy. "I want to take a look around. Something's going on. I can't put my finger on it. If I could see what's happening in the town—"

"What's to see but more Regians? One headquarters town is hardly different from another. That's one trouble with the military: little variety."

Since Mickle insisted, Las Bombas, finally, could only agree. They left their chambers and made their way downstairs through the bustling offices to the front of the town hall. Their horses, as far as Las Bombas could determine, had been stabled in an adjoining structure. Rather than raise questions, Mickle thought it best to leave their mounts and go on foot.

The guard at the doorway refused to let them pass. Despite the count's bluster and rattling of documents under the man's nose, the Regian stood firm. With utmost courtesy, he told Las Bombas that transient officers, by strict order of General Erzcour, were to remain in quarters.

"I don't much like that," muttered the count. "Confined to barracks? Officers on an important mission? That's an item I'll take up with Erzcour in the morning. The fellow's not only a traitor, he's discourteous to a brother officer. Besides, it gives me a sensation I've unfortunately learned to recognize over the years: It smacks of being under arrest."

Mickle hesitated, more than ever anxious to investigate the town. Las Bombas drew her away, warning that disregarding a general's orders could only lead to trouble. Reluctantly, she followed him back to their quarters.

Entering the room, Mickle was surprised to see a fair-haired girl bent over the saddlebags and belongings Las Bombas had left beside his bed. The girl straightened hurriedly and spun around.

"Here, here," cried Las Bombas, "what's all this?"

The girl, flustered for an instant, smiled and curtsied. "I'm the laundress, sir. I've come for your wash."

"Ah, and a charming little washerwoman you are," said Las Bombas, winking at her and playing every bit the gallant officer. "General Erzcour treats his guests well, I'll give him that much. Yes, my dear, I'd be glad to have a few things done up. You must get them back first thing in the morning, though. And go lightly on the starch."

"What are you up to?" demanded Mickle, stepping forward. "We didn't ask for a laundress."

"No, we didn't," said Las Bombas. "The general, I presume, wished to foresee our every need."

"And send someone rummaging through our bags?" Mickle eyed the girl sharply. "What are you after? More than shirts, I shouldn't wonder."

"Just tidying up," the girl protested, dropping another curtsy. "I wanted to change your bedclothes and put these old ones in the wash."

"Most thoughtful of you." The count beamed. "Now, Lieutenant, we must let this delightful creature go about her work."

"The sheets were fresh," said Mickle. "They didn't need changing."

"Eh?" Las Bombas blinked. "Ah, perhaps they were. Good. It's that much less for the delicate hands of this young lady."

Before the laundress could stop her, Mickle suddenly picked up the girl's basket and searched under the rumpled linen. "Here's your pistol. Mine, too."

"Tut, tut, that won't do." The count sternly eyed the girl. "Young women shouldn't play with firearms, let alone steal them. I'm beginning to think my comrade-in-arms has a point. You may be a laundress; you're certainly a thief—and perhaps more. You and I, my dear, must have a little talk about that."

The girl moved quickly, trying to dart out the door. The count seized her arm. The laundress twisted free, lost her balance, and stumbled back against the wall. Before Las Bombas could reach her, she snatched a dagger from under her shawl.

"Laundress, indeed!" cried the count. "First, she wants to do our wash, then tries to assassinate us!"

Mickle dropped the basket and flung herself on the girl, who struggled fiercely. The count ran to Mickle's aid. The laundress had nearly broken loose from Mickle's grasp.

"Hold her arm," ordered Mickle. "She's not trying to kill us. She's trying to kill herself."

The self-styled laundress would have succeeded in plunging the dagger into her own breast had not Mickle and Las Bombas borne her to the floor by sheer weight and strength. The count twisted the weapon from her hand and threw it aside.

The girl raised her head and glared defiantly. "Go on, kill me. Torture me. I don't care what you do."

"We're not going to do either," said Mickle. "But we're not letting you go until you tell us—"

The girl spat at her. "I'll tell you nothing. Damn you, all of you."

"Gently, there, my dear," said Las Bombas. "You don't seem too fond of Regians. That's understandable. As for the rest, you have some explaining to do."

The girl clenched her teeth. Mickled pulled her upright and sat her on the bed. "Listen to me," Mickle said quietly. "We're not too fond of Regians, either." For a moment, she was tempted to tell the girl who she was, but thought better of it. "We only want to help you."

"Liar!"

"Be calm, child," said Las Bombas. "We're not exactly whom you might suppose."

"You're Regians," the laundress flung back. "That's enough."

Las Bombas glanced at Mickle. "What now?"

Mickle put her hands on the girl's shoulders. "I want you to trust us, so I'm going to trust you. I'm going to tell you something, then you'll tell me why you were searching our rooms."

The laundress looked scornfully at Mickle, who continued: "We're on your side. There's more to it, but you don't need to know that. We're going to let you go. If we weren't your friends, we'd hardly do that, would we?"

"More lies. A trap—"

"No. All right, I can't expect you to believe us without proof. Do you know of Florian?"

"Everyone does."

"I've met him," said Mickle. "I can describe him to you. Not enough? I've met some of his friends, too. Do you know someone called Theo? A poet named Stock? What about Justin?"

The laundress paled. Mickle knew she had touched a deep nerve. "Justin. He was badly hurt once. I haven't seen him for a while, but I imagine he shows the signs of it. A red-haired girl, Zara. Another girl they talked about—"

"Rina," said the laundress. "Yes. I'm Rina. I believe you, but I can't understand— Who are you? Are you one of us?"

"Well—you might say so." Mickle smiled. "Yet I wouldn't go quite that far. We're all trying to help each other. Now, what do you have to say?"

It took Rina a few moments to collect her wits and accept the idea that her apparent enemies were, in fact, her friends. "The pistols— Yes, I wanted them. The townsfolk have been storing weapons. The Regians, when they came, tried to seize what was here. But we hid most of them: sabers, muskets, pistols. We have a fair stock; we can never have too much, of course. We steal what we can. We managed even to get hold of some grenades."

"It sounds to me," said Las Bombas, "that you've put together a nice little arsenal. What are you planning to do with it?"

"When the right time comes," answered Rina, "there's going to be an uprising. That's one secret the Regians haven't found out. Most of the townsfolk are in on it. So am I. When the signal's given, we'll be ready. But we have to choose the best moment. Once we come into the open, we'll have only one chance. We can't surprise the Regians twice. The reprisals will be terrible. So we've waited, hoping the queen's army would attack and advance up the valley. Then we'd risk our own attack. We're still waiting," Rina bitterly added. "A long time."

"I know," said Mickle. "I hope—well, I hope the war ends before you have to do anything."

"A conspiratorial laundress, eh?" said Las Bombas, "and a lovely one into the bargain."

"More than that," said Rina. "I work for the raiding parties up there in the hills. I pass along whatever I find out that could help them. You were new here. I thought you might have messages, special orders. I can't understand yet what's happening in Eschbach, but I know it's important. There've been a lot of troop movements; not many all at once, but they've been going on a good while, and more now. I haven't been able to get word to—to someone named Shrike. He's one of Florian's officers."

"Do you know anything of Theo?" Mickle asked. "I'd be glad for any news of him."

Rina shook her head. "I'm sorry. I don't want to say any more. Some things you don't need to know, either. I'd better go. They'll wonder what became of me."

"Don't forget my laundry," put in Las Bombas. "It not only needs washing, but it's a good excuse for you to come back. I'm to breakfast with Erzcour tomorrow. I'll winkle whatever I can out of him."

"I think I'd better have breakfast with him, too," said Mickle, as Rina hastily left them. "I want to hear for myself anything he might say. I'll take the chance. My hair's still short enough. There's no way I can manage a beard, but a little grime might answer. Besides, as you say, he won't pay any mind to a sub-lieutenant."

Las Bombas shook his head. "I'm not sure it's wise. Think it over. Best yet, sleep on it, which is exactly what I'm going to do."

Tired though she was, Mickle could not rest. She went to her chamber, but instead of trying to sleep, she stood again by the window. She had, finally, understood a part of what had troubled her. She was angry at herself for not realizing it immediately. The map of Westmark came into her mind as clearly as if it had been spread before her eyes.

She had, at first, assumed that Erzcour was sending fresh troops to reinforce the Regian divisions opposing her at Altus-Birkenfeld. The men and equipment she had seen, therefore, should have been moving west. Instead, it seemed they were bearing south.

# 17

He came full awake, like an animal: instantly, silently, with no wasted motion. Beck, one of the original company who had taken Rosana's place, roused him.

"Raven's here. Justin wants all officers."

Theo crawled out of his burrow. They had finally chosen a site above Eschbach. They must, he and Justin had decided, prepare now for winter. With luck, they could settle in and not move again for several months. The men had already started building durable shelters, dugouts and low huts, shored up with branches, roofed over with sod and patches of turf. Justin had ordered a larger structure for himself, to serve as command post and sleeping quarters, part dug into the side of a slope, the rest covered with twigs and limbs, like a half-finished beaver lodge.

Theo had been dreaming. He could not recapture what the dream had been, except it was pleasant. Now he only felt hungry, but he was used to that and knew it would grow worse. They had, for the time being, stopped most of their forays. Justin did not want to risk bringing attention to themselves or their whereabouts until they had a solid foothold. Food supplies, in consequence, had dwindled. Foraging lower down among the farms had become too dangerous. As Theo foresaw, there was almost no harvest. Justin had said he would deal with that. Theo had been content to leave it to him, impatient only to begin the raids again.

Beck strode beside him. The stars looked enormous. Theo glimpsed other figures moving toward Justin's lodge. "Did you tell the Monkey? I want him with us."

"He's not in camp."

Theo cursed between clenched teeth. The Monkey was scavenging again. He told Beck to warn the guard post. The Monkey must report immediately to Justin. He ducked through the entry. Justin and his other officers squatted in the wider section, maps on the ground in a wash of lantern light.

Luther glanced up. Theo could tell from his expression that it took the man a moment to recognize him. It puzzled Theo, this instant when Luther stared at him as a stranger. The scrub of beard covering Theo's cheeks, the layers of dirty clothing were no different in appearance from those of the rest of the company. Then Luther's face broke into a grin. He nodded, clearly glad to see him, yet there seemed an odd, regretful twist to his smile.

Beck had rejoined Theo. Justin was now aware of the Monkey's absence. Used to his ways, he never remarked on them. This time he looked angry. He said only: "Raven has bad news. We're to move."

Theo's heart sank, not only at the labor lost but as much at leaving his burrow. He had felt it was his first permanent home since they had gone into the Domitians. "When?"

"Now," Justin said. "We pull out altogether. That's from Florian."

"You had no idea?", said Luther. "Nothing from Rina?"

Justin shook his head. "We've been out of touch. This is the first we've stopped. She doesn't yet know where we are. I'll get word into Eschbach."

"I'll handle that," said Luther. "You can't lose time. You're needed elsewhere."

Luther bent over the map. "Florian's already sent a message to the queen, at Altus-Birkenfeld. We suspected something was astir a while ago. Now we're sure. Look here. Eschbach's at the head of the Sabrina valley, where it cuts southwest between the Domitians and—here—this long stretch of foothills. It's rough country. Once through it, though, it's flatlands northward to the Vespera. An easy road straight to Marianstat."

As Luther went on, Theo could guess what he would say. He did not want to hear it, let alone believe it.

"Erzcour's been given new divisions. He's sending all of them through the Sabrina valley. As far as we can tell, he's also moving troops out of Carlsbruch. No doubt he'll leave enough in place to keep Augusta from advancing. Most of his army, though, is going into the valley.

"He's gambling. It will be heavy going, but short going. What he loses in time, he'll more than make up after he's out. He can march on Marianstat with nothing to stop him.

"The queen will have to move all the troops she can spare. So will Florian. To—here." Luther put a finger on the map. "To La Jolie, one of the Montmollin estates.

"You're to join Florian there. It's a waste of time now trying to nip Erzcour's flank; a flea biting an elephant. Besides, he can afford sending up enough detachments to sweep out all of you. Florian needs you with him. He'll give you new orders at La Jolie."

Luther sat back on his heels. "That's all. We stop Erzcour at La Jolie and hold till winter, or it ends there."

"Can we do it?" Theo asked.

"I don't know. We've got no choice, do we? If you clear out fast enough, if you go through the foothills and keep ahead of Erzcour's advance guard, it's not impossible. We gamble, too. A small number travels faster than his heavy brigades."

Luther went on for a while, explaining details and answering questions from Justin and the officers. When it was over and they began filing out of the lodge, Luther took Theo's arm.

"A shame about Stock."

"Yes."

"The man taking his place. Kestrel. He's done well."

"Yes. I suppose so."

Luther looked at him for a long moment. "You're Kestrel, aren't you."

It was not a question, but a flat statement. At first, it surprised Theo. He hesitated an instant, then curtly nodded. He did not ask how Luther had known or how he had guessed. Luther said no more about it. To Theo, it seemed Luther had looked at him then with a terrible sadness.

The Monkey was back, standing in front of the lodge, laughing with some of the troopers as the meeting ended. The sky had begun to lighten. Their breath smoked as they chivvied one another and joked back and forth. Justin had stepped from the entry.

"You should have been here, Monkey," Justin said coldly. "I'll go over it all with you later. Get ready to move out. See to the cannon."

The Monkey gave an apologetic half-salute and bobbed his head. "Good thing I did better than usual. You'll be glad for extra rations if we're breaking camp again."

The man, Theo noticed, had put down two large sacks. He had already shared some of the contents with a couple of the troopers, who were gratefully munching away.

"I'd have tried for more, if I'd known," said the Monkey. "Bloody farm wench kicked up such a row. They're a shrewd lot. They've got who knows what-all squirreled away, and lie to your face and swear there's not another scrap in the house. Civilians! She had a good lesson, though."

The Monkey chuckled and winked. Theo halted. "What do you mean?"

The Monkey made a vague motion with his hands. Justin, who had been listening, came closer.

"You mind what you're about, Monkey," he said. "No more of this scavenging, not while we're on the march. You were out most of the night this time. That's already too much of a risk."

"I'd have been back long since," answered the Monkey, "if the damned Regian patrol hadn't come by." He grinned proudly. "They couldn't hold me long, not those lumpheads."

"You got caught?" Theo demanded. "Monkey, you're a damned fool. How did you get away?"

"Easy," said the Monkey. "Once we got to Eschbach—"

"They took you into Eschbach?" Justin broke in. "What then?"

"Why, Colonel, it wasn't anything, you know. They didn't give me any trouble."

Luther had come forward. "How long did they keep you there?"

"No time at all. I gave them the slip." The Monkey laughed and shook his head. "A sorry lot. Raw recruits."

"Lucky they let you keep the food," said Luther.

"It cost me some of it," said the Monkey. "A couple bottles of wine before they let me go."

"You said you gave them the slip," Theo put in.

"Yes, well, you see that was after they got done questioning me about—"

The Monkey stopped short and clamped his mouth shut. Justin's face went white. He seized the Monkey by the front of his jacket. "Questioned? What did you tell them?"

"Nothing!" blurted the Monkey. "Nothing! Colonel, I swear to heaven!"

Justin looked about to throttle him. The Monkey's eyes darted back and forth. It was the first time Theo had seen him show fear.

"Let be," ordered Luther, his face grave.

Justin relaxed his grasp.

"We have to make some sense of this," said Luther. "He was caught. He was questioned. We know that much. We don't know what, if anything, they got out of him."

The Monkey began swearing again that he had told nothing. "Only lies! Only a lot of rubbish! Those fools believe any kind of nonsense."

Luther spoke aside to Theo. "If he did talk, what could he have spilled? How much does he know?"

"He knows everything," said Theo, in growing alarm. "He knows where this camp is and how many of us. And—Luther, he knows that Rina's working for us in Eschbach."

This same realization had struck Justin. His scar clenched and unclenched, drawing up one side of his face. "Did you say the slightest word about Lapwing?"

"Not one!" The Monkey changed his tone to a sort of joking, cajoling plea. "Why, you know me better than that, Colonel. You've known me from the first. All we've been through—"

Justin did not reply. The Monkey rounded on Theo. "You know me, too. Very well do we know each other. Comrades. You couldn't have gotten by without me. That's a fact. I stayed with you, didn't I? Oh, we've seen each other in action. Side by side, close as brothers—"

"Yes," Theo burst out. "Yes, Monkey, we've been one and the same."

"We'll settle it once and for all," Justin said. "This is a court-martial, here and now. We three officers shall conduct it." He glanced at Theo. "What do you say?"

"If he's telling the truth, no harm done. If he's lying, he might have sold us out and Rina, too. We can't know for sure."

Justin turned to Luther. "You?"

"If you believe him, let him off with a reprimand," said Luther. "If you don't believe him, shoot him."

Justin was making an iron effort to control himself. If Theo had never seen the Monkey so fearful, he had never seen Justin so ravaged, his face livid, his hands shaking. His voice was cold and precise.

"I must take into account that this is one of my best men. I must take into account that we could not have done as well without him. I must take into account that, to my knowledge, he has never lied to me. I must take into account that he may be lying now."

Justin's voice rose to a high, strained pitch. "I must take into account that he might have betrayed us here. That he might have betrayed Rina—"

At the name, he faltered, almost unable to keep on. Until now, Theo had never imagined Justin loving anyone. Rina, he knew, loved Justin. That Justin felt as much for her had not occurred to him. Yet, Theo suddenly knew this was the case.

"Rina—" Justin was saying. "The possibility exists. Since it does, I can not afford the benefit of the doubt. Sentence of death—"

Before the words were out of Justin's mouth, the Monkey, cursing, spun around and flung himself past the nearby troopers. He ran full speed to the edge of the camp. Justin, eyes wild, raced after him.

The Monkey turned, hastily drew his pistol, and fired. The shot missed. The Monkey plunged into the undergrowth, Justin at his heels.

Stunned an instant, Theo dashed after them. He heard Luther call out but did not glance back. He shouldered his way through the bushes, twigs snapping in his face. The light was dim, he could barely make out the running figures ahead of him and went half blindly, following their sounds.

His boot caught on a dead branch. He went sprawling, the breath knocked out of him. In the time it took him to scramble up, Justin had distanced him. The Monkey, a clever woodsman, dodged among the trees. In other circumstances, the Monkey could have well outrun a pursuer. Justin, driven by sheer strength of will, was little by little closing the gap between them. As the woods thinned out, Theo caught sight of them again.

He was about to press on when he glimpsed something else and stopped short. The sky had brightened, and for an instant he thought it was the gleam of sun on the leaves. He saw now it was the glint of muskets. He shouted, but he was too distant, his warning unheard.

The Regian patrol opened fire. He saw the Monkey pitch forward and topple to lie motionless. Justin swung up his pistol, uncertain which way to turn as the Regians set upon him from both sides.

They had seized him and were dragging him off despite his struggling. Theo sprang ahead, half sobbing with despair. The patrol and their prisoner vanished into the undergrowth. He followed nevertheless until, moments later, he saw the Regians had untethered their horses. Justin, bound, had been flung across a saddle. The patrol was making for Eschbach.

Beaten, without hope of overtaking them, Theo turned and ran up the slope. Luther suddenly was in front of him, with some of the troopers. Theo gasped out what he had seen. Luther took his arm and roughly set him moving toward the camp.

Theo fought against him, shouting that they could not leave Justin, that they must get him back.

"Clear out of this," Luther snapped. "It's too late."

"He's alive. They're taking him to Eschbach." A further horror dawned on him. "If they question him? Torture him? He knows—"

"It doesn't matter," Luther said bluntly. You'll be gone. You can't help him, you can't help Rina."

"No. Damn you, Luther, I won't leave him."

"You will." Luther gripped him by the shoulders. "You're in command. You'll follow Florian's orders, hear? You'll do it now. Move out your people, Colonel Kestrel."

"Yes, I'm in command," Theo cried. "I'm a field commander, I'll follow Florian's orders as best I see them. We're going for Justin."

"You're mad. You'll lose the whole company."

"No. We can do it. The whole company won't go with me. Let half start for La Jolie. Beck will command them. The rest, with me. I want the cannon, too. Go with Beck. We'll catch up with you."

"You forget something," said Luther. "I'm not under your orders."

"Do as you please, then."

"You're not only a fool, you're a bad officer." Luther paused. "I'm attaching myself to your command." Then he grinned. "If you'd obeyed those orders, I'd have gone to Eschbach by myself."

# 18

The supreme commander was in excellent spirits, a condition remarkably different from his unpleasant days at the king's headquarters. Montmollin had gone; where and to do what did not interest Erzcour. The baron had become impossible. Erzcour, anguishing over joining the Regian staff, had spent many a sleepless night, and Montmollin had not appreciated the pain of his decision. Erzcour was relieved to see what he hoped was the last of him.

King Constantine, at the end of summer, had also become insufferable, meddling in military affairs that did not concern him and that he did not understand. Erzcour would have been happier if the king did not exist. Duke Conrad felt the same and had said as much. Erzcour and the duke dealt very well with each other. Erzcour disliked the man and had no doubt the feeling was mutual. At heart, they understood each other; which, perhaps, was the best reason for their dislike.

In any case, there had been important progress. He had been given all the supplies and troops he had asked for. The added units had allowed him to devise a new strategy, an excellent campaign plan. He had, at the duke's insistence, conferred with Cabbarus. The fellow had made some trivial suggestions, then tried to claim credit for the entire strategy. It was infuriating, but Erzcour put Cabbarus from his thoughts and devoted himself to his work, which he saw as a noble endeavor. Honor and loyalty, he had at last come to understand, must be taken in the broadest and most unselfish aspect. Serving Regia, he was most truly serving his country. By the end of the campaign, he would surely be carrying the baton of a field marshal.

The presence of his two visitors added zest to the general's morning, though he was glad that Captain Blossam's aide was not on his staff. He knew the sort: no doubt a younger son of excellent, perhaps noble, family; his commission bought, the war an amusement. Too fine of bone for a soldier, something of a slim dandy, a bit foppish, not altogether unlike Constantine. Erzcour deliberately ignored him. The excellent breakfast cleared away, Erzcour wished to hear details of Blossam's mission.

For his part, sweating with fear under his uniform, Las Bombas wished to say as little as possible and as quickly as possible. "Excellency, it is a matter of extreme sensitivity and delicacy."

"In other words: political," replied Erzcour. He disdained politicians and diplomats, and disdained even more those officers who considered themselves as such. It was, he felt, a corruption of their military duty.

"Say, instead, an affair of highest import." Las Bombas made a pretense of digestive relaxation, leaning back in his chair while he offhandedly continued. "I should prefer not to reveal it, even to Your Excellency, and only stress its urgency. I confess, sir, I did not expect to be restricted to quarters, commodious though they were."

"The restriction no longer applies. You are quite at liberty now. There was, naturally, a good reason for it."

"May one ask?"

"Of course." Erzcour felt expansive and indulgent, happy for the occasion to demonstrate the superiority of military maneuver over the diplomatic. "It was, essentially, a precaution. Secrets—even diplomatic ones—cannot be kept too long. But we must try. Indeed, Captain, the secret is quite open as of this instant, and will be soon quite clear to our enemies. To their despair, I am delighted to say."

Mickle, in her humble rank as Sub-Lieutenant Michael, bit her tongue. It was all she could do to keep silent while the count and Erzcour wasted time in politenesses. She was frightened, though not by fear of discovery. As the count promised, Erzcour had given her only the most casual scrutiny. During the night, however, bits had fallen one by one into place. She was by no means certain; she could only hope she was wrong.

"It is of true military elegance," Erzcour said. "In a word, Captain, we shall now proceed to win the war."

"Ah—as we all hope to do," said Las Bombas.

"Not by your methods, Captain," said Erzcour. "By honest soldiering."

Erzcour got up and went to his wall map. "Beautifully simple. You grasp it immediately, do you not? We march through the Sabrina valley. Once we strike easy terrain, we swing north past an estate called La Jolie. And from there to Marianstat."

Mickle's heart sank. Erzcour had, unwittingly, told her the last thing she needed to know. She had already understood the danger of a Regian thrust exactly as Erzcour described it. To do so, she also knew, depended on Regia's willingness to commit new divisions, at huge expense. Her only question: Would Regia accept such a burden? She had her answer. Her thoughts swung frantically between two points. She must be at the head of her army; she must reach Constantine. One or the other—she could not do both. She must be out of Eschbach immediately, though she feared it might be too late for either course.

Erzcour kept on, while Mickle went silently mad with impatience. "And so, you understand, Captain, I wished simply to keep transient officers—indeed, all officers even of field grade—from committing indiscretions of conversation with civilians, especially with the charming ladies of Eschbach. This is no longer necessary. Our movements are well in train, nothing can stop them. In addition, even more importantly, I chose to avoid the risk of officers' being captured by these gangs of bandits and terrorists that so plague us. They would not hesitate to torture a captive for any information they might gain. We have proof. They are savages, they obey no rules of decent, civilized warfare.

"The infamous Kestrel, for example. He is the most abominable, ruthless—no, he shares that distinction with another we know to be called Shrike. They shall be rooted out, to the last of them."

Erzcour went back to his desk. "Would you care to

see a real live terrorist? It would be an education for you lofty diplomatic warriors. We caught one last night. Then we let him go."

"An unusual act of mercy," said Las Bombas. "But if he is no longer here—"

"We do not show mercy to their sort. We have our little games, too." Erzcour chuckled. "Yes, we caught this fellow looting, a crime in itself. We persuaded him to see reason, and set him on his way again. We planned for him to show us where Shrike had set up new headquarters; not for immediate action, but rather like playing a fish. The fellow was to rejoin his gang and report back to us from time to time. Whether he would have kept his word is open to question. We shall never know. He met, you see, with a misadventure.

"To make up for it, we have an even better specimen. It may well be Shrike himself, we are not certain. We are, shall I say, in process of determining that. Come along, Captain. And your aide. It will be all the more salutary and instructive for the young gentleman."

Neither Mickle nor Las Bombas had time to consider the general's invitation. Erzcour had already taken the count's arm, conducting him from the office to the end of the corridor and down a few steps, with Mickle following, struggling to compose herself.

The general ushered them into one of the archive chambers now serving as an interrogation room. The single window had been heavily coated with black paint, the cabinets rearranged to make room for a writing table and bench. Papers were heaped in the corner, bits of food strewn on the floor. A sour smell hung in the room, where a soldier was mopping away a puddle of water. Two officers in shirt sleeves stood beside the man bound to a chair.

The Regians stiffened to attention at sight of Erzcour, who took one of the candles from the table and went to the prisoner. The man was unconscious, his head lolled.

"Gentlemen, let me present our guest." Erzcour beckoned to Las Bombas and Mickle. "A discourteous one; it seems he has decided to take a nap."

One of the officers reported that the man refused to answer questions. Erzcour shrugged. "He will." He turned to the count. "It will follow a pattern. First, insolent refusal. Bravado—for a while. Sooner or later, he will answer everything and give us even more than we ask. They all do, you know. A matter of time and patience. In this case, we wish to shorten the time. Our patience, too, is short."

Erzcour raised the man's face. Despite the bruises and the tangle of clotted hair covering the brow, Mickle recognized Justin immediately. She nearly cried out. Las Bombas paled and made a small sound in his throat.

"Unsettling to you?" Erzcour smiled and shook his head. "We conduct our own fashion of diplomacy here. I assure you, we shall have more truth out of this fellow than ever came from a minister of state.

"Can you rouse him?" Erzcour asked the officer. "Captain Blossam would appreciate the opportunity of posing a few questions of his own. He might have better success. You, evidently, have had none whatever."

The officer flinched under his commander's eye and motioned for the soldier to pick up the water bucket. At that moment, Erzcour's adjutant came into the room.

"Eh? What's this about?" asked Erzcour. The adjutant drew his chief aside and whispered hastily in his ear. Erzcour's good spirits evaporated, his face turned a dull red. His subordinate continued murmuring something Mickle strained uselessly to hear. Erzcour slammed the candleholder down on the table.

"Absurd! This goes too far! Insufferable!" He turned to Las Bombas. "Like all families, our military household has its occasional inconveniences. One of them is about to happen. I must attend to it. Return, please, to my office. I shall rejoin you shortly."

Mickle would have hung back as Erzcour stamped out of the room. Las Bombas pulled her away, muttering, "Do as he says. Nothing else for it at the moment."

With Mickle racking her brain and insisting they could not leave Justin as he was, they hurried down the corridor. "Poor devil," murmured the count. "I see no help for him. Your idea's blown sky-high, too. Start back now. With everything else astir, we'll be lucky to reach Altus-Birkenfeld."

"I have to think it out," said Mickle. "There's too much all at once. Witz is there, he'll do his best—"

Rina had suddenly come around the corner and hurried up to them. Her face was mottled, her eyes puffy. She made a show of looking through her laundry basket, and the passersby saw nothing but the unremarkable sight of a laundress taking up some matter of business with two Regian officers.

"He's alive," Mickle said hastily before Rina could speak. "Yes, I know it's Justin. We saw him."

"They'll torture him." Rina was half sobbing. "They'll kill him, finally, no matter what."

"Hush, hush," put in Las Bombas. "You'll have people staring." He raised his voice. "Yes, my dear, in the matter of shirts—"

"He's told them nothing," Mickle said to Rina. "Worst is they have the idea he might be—what did they call him—Shrike."

"He is!" Rina cried. "Don't you understand? He's the commander—"

"Keep your voice down," muttered Las Bombas. "Ah, yes. The question of starch—"

"My friends told me he was brought here," said Rina. "We've tried to find a plan. They're willing. They'll get him free somehow. We're ready, all of us. I can give the word."

"Do nothing," Mickle ordered. "Not right now. Do you hear me?" Rina, she saw, was in a terrible state. "Listen. When Erzcour comes back, I'll ask to see Justin again. I don't know what I'll do. At least I'll be on hand. I'll manage to keep them from doing worse to him."

She broke off. The adjutant had appeared, surprised to find them still in the hall. Las Bombas stammered an excuse about his wash. The adjutant led them to Erzcour's office.

"Insanity," cried Las Bombas as soon as the door had closed. "Little fool! She'll set the whole town by the heels. For the sake of one man? She's gone mad."

"No," said Mickle. "She's simply in love with him."

"Worse!" groaned Las Bombas. "Who knows what folly she'll commit! Gracious heaven, she told us herself: Once the townsfolk show their hand, it's do or die—and die in any case. Yes, they might get him out. What then? It's the end for all of them."

Las Bombas clamped his mouth shut. Erzcour had

come in. The general's temper had not improved. No sooner had he sat down than Mickle, to the count's dismay, spoke up.

"What? What, sir, have you to say?" Erzcour turned his annoyance on this junior officer who had ventured to address him directly and without permission.

"Sir, concerning your prisoner—"

"My aide was greatly impressed," Las Bombas put in. "He wishes to observe further."

"Ah?" Erzcour raised his eyebrows. "I had thought it might be strong meat for the lieutenant's stomach. Perhaps, after all, there is hope for him. Yes, of course. It will be all the more instructive now. I have summoned a most excellent individual, an expert in these cases. I, too, hope to see truly professional methods. Excuse me, Captain, for a few moments."

Erzcour began scribbling a rapid succession of memoranda. He was still writing when his adjutant ushered in a new visitor. In modestly drab but well-tailored clothing, the man was short and dumpy. He carried a soft hat in one hand; in the other, a black leather case. The count's jaw dropped. Horrified, he turned wide eyes on Mickle, whose face had gone ashen.

It was Skeit. Hardly glancing at two minor officers, the little man went straight to Erzcour and bobbed his head in a cheerfully familiar but most unmilitary greeting. Erzcour put down his pen.

"Here we are, sir," Skeit began. "Soonest possible. I took a little while choosing all I thought was needed—tools of the trade, as you might say. It saves running back for some little item one might overlook. More haste, less speed, as it were."

"Yes, yes," Erzcour said impatiently. "It's your business, not mine."

"As you say, sir." Skeit winked a pink-rimmed eye. "We all have our specialities."

"I hope to join you later," said Erzcour. "It would be gratifying to see a craftsman at work. We still have something to learn from fellows like you. Meantime, these officers will observe your methods. Unless, of course, you have your little professional secrets."

"Only skill, nothing secret," answered Skeit. "I shall be honored."

Erzcour waved a hand. "Captain Blossam. His aide."

Skeit bowed. "Gentlemen. Now, if you'd be kind enough to follow me." Skeit turned away, then turned back again, frowning. He shook his head, blinked for a moment.

"General," Skeit declared, "these are not Regian officers." He motioned with his head toward Las Bombas. "This one—"

"How dare you!" cried Las Bombas. "You mistake yourself, sir, and impugn me at the same time, you detestable weasel!"

Had there been doubt at all in Skeit's mind, the count's outburst settled it. "Spies! Arrest them, sir. Instantly!"

Erzcour had jumped to his feet. That same moment, his window shattered under a volley of musketry. Mickle cried out. There was sharp firing in the street. Shouts of alarm rang in the corridor. Erzcour, without question or hesitation, snatched a pistol from his desk.

Before he could aim, Rina burst through the door. Behind her, the corridor was in an uproar. Shots rattled down the hallway. Some of the armed townspeople had already forced their way into the building. Rina halted no more than a second. Seeing Erzcour with pistol raised, she sprang forward and threw herself on him. Erzcour, under the sudden assault, stumbled back, his weapon discharging in air.

Mickle and Las Bombas ran to help the laundress struggling with Erzcour. Skeit, quick as an adder, darted ahead of them. His arm scarcely seemed to move. A thin blade shot from his sleeve into his hand. Rina whimpered and fell back. Shouting in rage, Las Bombas seized the pudgy man by the throat. Skeit drove his knee into the count's belly and sprang away.

Mickle dropped to her knees beside Rina. The girl stared at her, unseeing. With a cry, Mickle turned from the body and struck at Erzcour, who had begun reloading his pistol.

That same instant, a townsman with a musket leaped over the body of the adjutant in the doorway. Others followed. The first fired point-blank at Erzcour, then ran forward, clubbing the general with his musket even before he fell.

Skeit had vanished. Las Bombas seized Mickle, roaring for her to get out. The townsmen had fallen on Erzcour, striking at him with their musket butts. One of the men, turning away for a moment, sighted Mickle and the count, and shouted for his comrades.

"Run for it!" bellowed Las Bombas. "They think we're Regians!"

# 19

Luther had insisted. While half the company, under Beck, set out for La Jolie, the gray-haired Raven refused to hear any protest from Theo.

"I'll go to Eschbach first," Luther told him. "Alone. I know the town. You don't. I can find out where they're keeping him. The town hall is my best guess. But exactly where? He may not be alive. In which case"—Luther grimaced and shook his head—"in which case, you'll drop the whole business and get on your way as fast as you can."

"And if he's alive?" Theo's horse was already saddled. Theo had slung a musket over his shoulder. He stood beside Luther, shivering a little in the cold dawn.

"We'll see. I'll get back as soon as possible. We'll decide then."

"Rina? If she's in danger, I want her out of there."

"If possible."

"It will be. We'll make it so."

Though Luther had insisted on following his own course, Theo was firmly set on the rest of the plan. He and his part of the company would halt as close to Eschbach as they dared. Thus, Luther could rejoin them without delay.

"You'll lose hours if you come back here," said Theo. "We'll wait for you as long as it takes. I can be in position almost at the outskirts of town."

"Broad daylight? If you're attacked?"

"That will be my affair."

The cannon had been hitched to the limber, the company was ready. Theo signaled them to move out. Luther objected no further. However, as they started from the hills, Theo sensed that the older man would have preferred his own solitary methods. They said little to each other along the way. Luther's face was hard, he seemed caught up in his thoughts. The sun had come out, it would be a bright day.

Theo felt almost lighthearted, the same giddiness coming over him as it did at the outset of each raid. He was glad for Luther's help, though he would have done no differently without it.

He wished only one thing: for the Monkey to be alive and with him.

Everything suddenly changed. Near Eschbach, Theo imagined that he heard firing. It puzzled him. It could hardly be possible; yet, the closer they came, the louder the sound. Finally, it was unmistakable. He and Luther rode forward until they had a clear sight of the town. Theo pressed his eye to the spyglass. After a moment, he handed over the glass.

"See for yourself. They're fighting in the streets."

Luther squinted in turn. A look of joy and bewilderment had come over his face. "Lunatics! Insurrection? Fools! They can't hold. They'll be wiped out. It's madness—heaven help them, but what great madness! There go your plans, lad. What now?"

"Now? We support them."

He did not wait for Luther's reply, he did not hear if Luther made one. He did not even remember giving the signal to his company. There was only the horse straining under him, the hoofbeats jolting, and the screaming in his ears. These were Kestrel's people behind him. They had begun their cry as they galloped into the heart of the town.

He had lost track of Luther. In the square, when Theo sprang from the saddle, he glimpsed him again. Luther had run toward an overturned wagon serving as makeshift barricade and strong point at the near side of the square.

The cannon, finally, had come rattling over the cobbles, the horses drawn up, rearing. He shouted for the gunners to unlimber it. One wing of the town hall was ablaze. From a window, a bulky shape dangled awkwardly at the end of a rope. It appeared to be wearing a general's uniform. The face was covered with bright splotches like scarlet flowers.

Luther had come back, beside him a heavyset man with a bush of red hair over a powder-streaked face. A tradesman of some sort, he had kept his apron on; a red ribbon, the ends long and loose, was tied around his arm. The streamers gave him a festive look.

"Colonel, have your men direct some fire there—" He pointed to the upper stories of the town hall. "We have most of the ground floor, but a lot of Regians are holding out in the tower. They're shooting down at our people."

"Tell the gunners what you want," Theo said. "Tell them I ordered it."

"He thinks they'll soon have Justin," Luther said. "He's alive, in an interrogation room. They're trying to break him out through a window."

"Rina?"

"They found her body. They'll try to bring it out, too."

With a cry of rage, Theo started for the wagon, motioning some of the company to follow. The sudden roar of the cannon made his ears sing. The gunners crowed as a corner of the tower crumbled. Another ball hit more squarely. They reloaded and continued firing until the redheaded tradesman waved his arms for them to train the piece on a Regian troop galloping from a side street.

Theo crouched by the wagon. At the housefronts around the square, he glimpsed what seemed at first to be heaps of rags. He noticed, then, red armbands fluttering from them.

Justin's fieldpiece was proving its worth. The Regian attack had broken before the gunners exhausted their ammunition. Some of the Regians, however, had dashed into the buildings to continue firing from the upper windows. At the opposite corner, in the shadow of the town hall itself, a band of townspeople exchanged sharp volleys with a squad of foot troops. Despite the cover of another wagon and a hastily made breastwork of lumber, the townsmen were hard pressed and could not advance. Theo motioned for his company to reinforce them. He unslung his musket. He and Luther dashed across the square.

He caught sight, then, of a few men running from behind the building, among them a pale-haired figure. He shouted for his men to quicken their fire to keep the Regians from turning musketry on Justin and his fleeing rescuers. A bullet sang past Theo's head, another splintered the wagon shaft as he stepped away from the breastwork, beckoning to Justin.

The Regian fire slackened. Theo's marksmen were taking their toll. Justin, gasping, scrambled over the wagon. He stared at Theo.

"Damn you!" Justin shouted. "Damn you! What have you done?"

Instead of gratitude, Justin's anger struck Theo full in the face and, bewildered, he could only stammer, "We came for you—"

"You had orders. You should have gone."

"I wasn't going to leave you here," Theo flung back. "They'd have tortured you."

"They did. You thought I'd have broken? No. I told them nothing. I never would, no matter what they did. Fool! You could have lost the whole company. How many lost now?"

Justin's violet eyes blazed out of the mass of bruises. He gave a cry like a hurt animal. "Rina's dead! Do you know that? She's dead! If you'd followed orders—"

"The uprising had already started. It wasn't our doing. We'd have saved her if we could. We knew the danger. Luther knew it. He'd have tried to get you out, no matter."

Luther had not spoken. Theo turned to him. The gray-haired man was leaning against the wagon, his head resting on the wooden shaft. His leathery face was calm, but his eyes were blank. There was no sign of a wound.

Only when Theo ran to him did he see the stain spreading over his shirtfront.

Theo's fury at the sight rose higher than Justin's. He ran to the corner of the breastwork, he would have thrown himself bare-handed against the Regian troops. His rage found its target.

From a wing of the town hall, two Regian officers had galloped their horses into the square and turned sharply away, heading for a side street. Theo brought up his musket and fired.

One of the Regians slumped forward in the saddle as the horse plunged on. The second officer's mount shied, reared, and pitched its rider to the ground.

Theo flung away the musket and drew his saber. He was upon the man before the Regian regained his feet. He swung up the blade. The Regian twisted around, arms raised against the blow.

Theo halted the stroke in midair. The blade fell from his hands. He stared into the terrified face of Count Las Bombas.

In the moment it took the count to recognize him, Theo had pulled him to his feet. Las Bombas paid no heed to Theo's blurted questions.

"Mickle!" shouted Las Bombas. "It was Mickle!"

Theo at first understood nothing. The count brought his face closer. "She's with me! We were escaping. You shot her!"

Theo staggered at the count's words. His rage vanished, driven out by the new horror of what he had done. Everything around him turned to nightmare. The stench of old blood caught in his throat. He saw Stock's body again, and the Monkey, the kestrel's shrieking rang in his ears. All of it had brought him to this and had, finally, swept away even Mickle.

Justin had followed. "No prisoners. Kill him. Have done."

Theo rounded on him. "It's Las Bombas. You know him. He was here with Mickle. I may have killed her."

Justin still did not comprehend. Las Bombas had caught the reins of his horse and was urging Theo to hurry.

Theo ran back to where he had left his mount. Las Bombas, in the saddle, set his horse between Theo and Justin.

"Listen to me!" cried Las Bombas. "We had to dress as Regians. The queen was on her way to Mull. Queen Augusta, don't you understand? She could be badly hurt. Or killed—"

"Not the only one," Justin flung back. "Queen? What do I care for any of her like!"

The redheaded tradesman, apron spattered, had come up with some of his comrades. "We have the town. It's ours now."

Justin spun around. "You have nothing. Yours? You can't hold it. They'll send reinforcements."

"Yes, but we'll hold it awhile." The man grinned bleakly. "We're all dead men, I know that. There's a troop on the way. We'll stand them off a time. Enough to let you take your men out. You can't help us, but we can help you."

Theo, mounted, rode to the count's side. Justin snatched at the reins. "You follow orders. Get your people together."

"You're in command again," Theo cried. "Take them

out yourself. You don't need me. I'm going after Mickle."

Justin made an enormous effort to control himself. His voice was ice. "You know what this means. Desertion under fire. Court-martial. I'll overlook it if you start this instant for La Jolie. You don't understand what you're doing."

"I understand exactly what I'm doing." Theo wheeled his horse. Leaving Justin in the square, he galloped in the direction Mickle had taken, Las Bombas beside him.

Hoping she had halted only a little distance away, Theo cast an eye into every corner. He saw no riderless horse, no sign of Mickle. The firing had started again.

As far as he could judge, Mickle had not gone toward the high Domitians, but westward out of Eschbach into the foothills. He pressed on, Las Bombas heaving and panting behind him. His horse was lathered by the time they reached the first fringe of woodland. The count begged him to halt and reined up his own mount.

The stretch of woods lay bare and empty. Theo strained his ears for some sound among the dead leaves. "She's gone farther. She'll have to stop somewhere."

Las Bombas had begun stripping off his Regian tunic. "This wretched thing nearly cost our lives in the town hall. They took us for Regians there, it was all we could do to outrun them. Then, you!"

"How could I know? I kill Regians."

"You kill uniforms!" retorted Las Bombas. His face softened. He looked sadly at Theo. "I'm sorry. You couldn't help it. Yes, my boy, we'll find her. Give me a moment. I'm not quite over the shock, seeing you this way.

"I couldn't believe my eyes," Las Bombas went on. "My dear boy, I hardly knew you. You looked like a madman. I could have taken you for—why, even for that bloodthirsty fellow, Kestrel."

"I am Kestrel," Theo said. "No. I was Kestrel."

# 20

Weasel had recovered, but Sparrow still worried about him, a new sensation for her. Before, as much as he had exasperated her and tried her patience, she had never been seriously anxious about his well-being. Weasel had never been ill a day in his life.

Soon after they had witnessed the burning of the great house, he had fallen sick; Sparrow could not imagine what ailed him. He seemed feverish, yet his brow did not feel hot or even especially warm to her touch. The two water rats had fled into the woods that night, hiding there as if pursued by something monstrous, terrifying, and nameless. Weasel, despite the comfortable nest Sparrow made for him in the underbrush, tossed fitfully and slept little; when he did sleep, he whimpered and yelled and ended by waking himself up.

Sparrow tended him as best she could. She had stolen ample food. Weasel refused it. She realized he must be sick indeed, but had no idea what to do for him. She continued her medical treatment, which consisted of sitting by him day and night, watching silently, and stroking his hair to soothe him when he turned restless.

Suddenly, he recovered. One morning, he roused, looked around, and demanded something to eat. He wolfed down all the provisions Sparrow had been saving. He was his old self again; but not entirely, and this was what worried her. His narrow face had a sallow cast, he was thinner, he looked more than ever like his namesake. Even after he was up and around, and as aggravating as he had always been, he seemed peaky. Sometimes an odd, haunted look came into his eyes.

If only they could find Keller, Sparrow believed, all would be well. She did not understand why she felt so miserable without him, suffering in ways she could not describe, since it was unclear to her why she was suffering in the first place. She only knew it was necessary to find him. When Weasel showed signs of tiring or drew, frightened, into himself, she talked to him about Keller and he always cheered up, as if he were listening to a marvelous fairy tale.

They continued eastward through woodlands and gently sloping hills, trudging hand in hand. Had they been less ingenious, they would have starved. Had they been more imaginative, they would have seen the impossibility of their goal and given it up. Being merely practical, they dealt with whatever came to hand.

They adapted the scavenging methods from their old days in The Fingers. Instead of combing the inlets for whatever the river brought, or rowing into the port of Marianstat, they navigated over land into small farms and hamlets, begging or stealing what they could. Sometimes they met with disappointment. Reaching a village, they occasionally found it deserted, the houses charred and gutted. This became more often the case as they continued farther east. Sometimes they left empty-handed, having no wish to search closer; for they both, unlike themselves in the past, had developed a distaste for dead bodies. Weasel, especially, now shunned them. On their boldest forays, they crept into Regian encampments. There, danger was greatest; but so were the pickings.

It began turning chilly at night. It occurred to Sparrow that they must find something better than sheltering in thickets. She wanted a more permanent base where she could accumulate provisions for the winter, where they could return at the end of a day: What she wanted, simply, was a home.

In time, she found the spot: a fair-sized chamber formed by a tumble of rocks. The water rats added dead limbs entwined with smaller branches to make a roof and a rough screen at the chamber's entry. What attracted them was not only the cavelike shelter but, still more, its closeness to a large town, the largest they had seen since leaving Marianstat. It would be their treasure mine, their hunting ground. It was full of Regians, which made it all the better. Sparrow had quickly learned that Regians enjoyed supplies of every kind; the enemy was always ripe for plucking. She did not know the name of the town, and it did not interest her. It would have meant nothing even had she known it was called Eschbach.

They decided, next morning, to survey it. They set out happily, as if their fortune awaited them. Closer to Eschbach, Weasel grew terribly agitated. Sharp exchanges of firing were coming from the town; underlying them, the deep roar of explosions. Black smoke had overcast the clear sky. Weasel began to shake, his face puckered. Since his illness, loud noises upset him. Sparrow feared he might go strange again. She took his hand and led him back, calculating that they might venture into the town later when it quieted.

They had not gone any distance when she stopped and motioned Weasel to leave off his whimpering. What had caught her eye was a white horse, saddled and bridled, tethered to a shrub. The prospect delighted her, new vistas opened. The horse would serve as transport; as a pack animal, it would allow them to carry off enormous amounts of plunder. Weasel forgot his distress and brightened.

Only then did Sparrow notice a figure sitting on a boulder. From the uniform, she recognized it as a Regian officer. She counted this another stroke of luck. She had learned from experience that officers were richer than common soldiers. The Regian had not heard them approach. He sat hunched over, head between his knees. He looked as if he had just been sick.

The water rats crept up silently. Weasel, careless, stepped on a dry twig. The Regian turned, staring bewildered. For that passing instant, Sparrow saw in his face the same haunted look that so troubled her in Weasel. The officer made a vague defensive motion with his hand and tried to get up. By then, it was too late. Sparrow and Weasel were upon him.

Their onslaught shook him out of his numbness. The officer, though slender, proved strong. They wrestled him back and forth; he tried to shake them off, but they clung doggedly. The officer succeeded, at one moment, in flinging Weasel aside. The Regian had only assured his own defeat. Weasel returned to the charge. He clenched his fist into a hard, tight ball and punched the officer squarely in the nose.

The Regian sat down, choking and snuffling, his nose bleeding a river. Sparrow and Weasel seized the chance to rip away the braids decorating his tunic and use them as cords. The Regian now offered only the feeblest resistance. Within moments, his arms were securely bound. He slumped dejected, stunned by more than Weasel's fist, for the spirit had entirely gone out of him.

The water rats began searching him, turning out his pockets, rummaging in his tunic. They were extremely disappointed at finding nothing whatever. His boots were too big for either of them, but they could salvage his clothes; and there was always the horse.

Weasel, nevertheless, was vexed. The officer, he decided, must be hiding something, and he began searching him again.

"Let me alone," said the officer. "I never carry money."

"You might know," Weasel told Sparrow. "When we get a Regian, it's a poor one."

"If you're after money," said the captive, "you can have all you want."

"What good is it here?" said Sparrow. "Food's what we need."

"You'll have that, too. Let me go. You'll be given whatever you ask."

Sparrow had a better chance to observe her prize. He was younger than she had first thought. His attempt at a moustache was pitiful. There was also something definitely wrong with him, though he had no wound except the one Weasel had bestowed on him. The firing had started again, much louder. The Regian flinched as if he had been struck.

"We'll let you go after you pay up, not before," Sparrow said. "If you can get us all you say, I want my eye on you."

"I'll give you my parole."

"What's that?" asked Weasel. "Do you have it on you?"

"It's a rule of war," said the young Regian. "If an officer's captured, he gives his parole he won't try to escape. He gives his word."

"I want better than that," said Sparrow. "Come on, we'll take you into town. We'll stay with you until we get our pay."

"Ransom," said the young officer. "That's what it's called."

"Whatever you call it," said Weasel, "we want it. Come on."

"No—not now." The officer had paled. "They're still fighting. No, I can't go there now. Wait. It has to end."

Sparrow suddenly realized something. "You're afraid, aren't you? You're a coward."

The Regian did not answer. Sparrow was satisfied she had understood his difficulty. "Good for you. Keller says most people are. He says it shows common sense."

The Regian, even so, was turning out to be more problem than prize. It now occurred to her that if she and Weasel took the Regian into the town, his friends might simply snatch him away. She could send Weasel to bargain with the Regians while she guarded the prisoner; but she was reluctant to let her brother go alone. There was no telling what might happen to him, especially if the fighting started again. The safest course was to bring the captive to the shelter and keep him there until she had a better idea. With Weasel leading the horse, she prodded the officer along to the cave.

The young man seemed grateful to have any sort of roof over his head, though little interested in the food Sparrow offered. She and Weasel agreed it was best to keep him tied, despite his promise; so she was obliged to feed him mouthful by mouthful. That he was Regian made no difference to her. Had he been dead, she would have picked his pockets. As he was sick, she tended him.

Weasel, having overcome his disappointment, was fascinated. It was the first time he had talked with a Regian. This one seemed no different from anyone else. Weasel asked his name. The officer hesitated.

"You may call me—yes, I suppose you may as well call me Connie."

"You should be fighting," said Weasel. "What are you doing here?"

The officer did not reply for a time. He appeared to be under a heavy burden.

Finally, as if it were the only way to lift it from himself, he blurted out: "Have you ever fought? Have you seen a battle? I hadn't, not until today. I was riding into town with my escort—with friends—when it started. The enemy—you people—had a cannon. They fired into us. My aide was next to me. The cannonball—"

The Regian broke off. Sparrow feared he would be sick, burst into tears, or do both.

"You ran away?" said Weasel. "I don't blame you."

"It was despicable, cowardly," said Connie. "I couldn't help it. I never knew what it would really be like. I didn't want to run. It just happened of itself. You won't tell anybody, will you?"

"It's no business of mine," said Sparrow. "Besides, I don't think it's—whatever you said it was. You don't seem a bad sort, for a Regian."

"You don't hate me?"

"Why should I?" said Sparrow. "I hardly know you."

The young Regian looked at her for a long time. "You're an odd sort of girl. Quite remarkable for a commoner."

"She's very common," put in Weasel, "but not remarkable."

"Do you live in the woods?" the Regian asked. "Do you have some occupation?"

"We're looking for Keller," said Weasel. "Do you know where he is? He's teaching us to be scriveners. I used to be a thief, but not anymore."

The captive had dropped into his own thoughts. Weasel, exhausted by his day, curled up and went to sleep. Sparrow stayed wakeful. The Regian had closed his eyes, but soon turned restless. Sparrow treated him as she had treated Weasel, stroking his forehead, talking to him gently when he woke in alarm.

Once, during such a spell, more asleep than awake, the prisoner sat up and stared past her as if trying to make out something at a great distance. Sparrow soothed him and he lay back again.

Before he slept, in a tone of astonishment at himself, he said: "Do you know—I used to play with toy soldiers."

Weasel could not believe his good luck. Regians were practically raining down on him. Next morning, he caught another.

Sparrow had decided that Weasel should first spy out the town. He was not to go into Eschbach, but only see if the fighting had stopped. Then they would discuss matters with Connie, who had somewhat recovered from his terror of the day before.

Weasel, then, had set out armed with Connie's saber, which was too heavy for him, and Connie's cap, which was too big for him. Hardly out of sight of the cave, Weasel glimpsed another Regian stumbling toward him, leading another horse. This Regian looked in much worse case than Connie. One side of the officer's tunic was bloodstained, and he seemed hardly able to keep to his feet.

Yelling for Sparrow, Weasel brought up the saber, which he had been carrying over his shoulder, and charged: an onrush made slower than he intended owing to the cumbersome blade. What he lacked in speed, Weasel made up in ferocity, shouting horribly and making warlike grimaces: to such good effect, he chose to believe, that the new arrival was frightened out of of his wits. In any case, the officer fell down.

Sparrow, by this time, had joined her brother. At first, she thought the new Regian had died. He had only fainted and, after a few moments, was able to walk unsteadily, supported on either side by the water rats.

"Here's a new one," Weasel announced as they brought in their second trophy. "I got him myself."

The effort had been too much for the already weakened captive, who fainted once more. Sparrow beckoned to Connie: "You'd better come and see. He's worse off than you are."

"Untie me, then."

Sparrow hesitated. She was not certain she wanted two loose Regians on her hands, even though one was unconscious.

"Parole," said Connie. "I promise."

"All right. Parole." She nodded to Weasel, who undid the makeshift ropes. "Do you know what to do when someone's hurt like that?"

"Not really," admitted Connie. "I remember there was a hunting accident once in—where I'm from. They called a physician."

"You're no help." Sparrow snorted.

"It's a bullet wound." Connie had bent over the motionless figure. "The first thing to see is whether it's come out. Yes, this one has."

"Do you know him?" asked Weasel.

"No. In fact, it's a girl."

Weasel blinked. "Are you sure?"

Sparrow pushed her brother out of the way. She was about to lend Connie a hand when the screening of the shelter was ripped away. Weasel jumped for his saber. Sparrow clapped a hand over her mouth to stifle a scream at the bearded, begrimed shape staring at her. It was hardly a man.

She decided it was a monster.

# 21

Theo and the count had searched as far into the woods as the day allowed, continuing past nightfall, when even Theo admitted it was useless. They rested awhile and started back toward Eschbach. Theo had first assumed that Mickle had ridden deep into the foothills. He wondered if he had miscalculated. She had, perhaps, gone to earth somewhere closer to the town, and he had overreached her. They began once more quartering the ground they had so hastily passed through. It was then he glimpsed two horses tethered beside a tumble of branches. Las Bombas recognized one as Mickle's. The white steed was a Regian cavalry mount.

Mickle, Theo feared, might have fallen into enemy hands. So it appeared when he broke into the shelter and saw one figure on the ground, a Regian hussar bending over it. Paying no mind to what looked like a pair of ragged goblins, he threw himself on the officer.

"Stop it! Stop!" cried one of the goblins. "It's only Connie!"

Las Bombas had dropped to his knees beside Mickle. "She's alive."

The hussar showed no desire to fight. Theo flung him aside. Las Bombas had already begun examining Mickle's wound. Theo's musket ball had passed cleanly through the flesh; no ribs had been broken, but she had lost much blood. Theo would have lifted her up but Las Bombas waved him off.

"She'll be all right, my boy. I'll tend to her. It's one of my professions. If only I had my elixirs and potions—"

"You know they're worthless."

"Yes," admitted the count, "but better than nothing."

The hussar, escorted by the goblins, ventured closer to Theo. Sparrow stepped between them.

"Connie's our prisoner," she said. "We'll get a ransom for him. He's given his parole."

"That's true," said the hussar. "Who you may be, I have no idea. I assume you observe the rules of warfare."

"As much as you do," Theo said.

Las Bombas had shifted his attention from Mickle to the hussar. He stared and climbed to his feet. Theo had never seen the count so taken aback. Las Bombas squinted, frowned, and shook his head. The hussar had drawn away. Las Bombas went up to him.

"You, sir! Who the devil are you?"

The hussar did not reply. Las Bombas took the officer's face in one hand and turned the youth's head sideways. "I don't believe what I see," he called to Theo. "Look at that profile. I've seen it a thousand times—no, alas, not so often—on Regian gold pieces. That's royalty."

The officer pulled away. Las Bombas snatched a saber from the ground. "If you aren't King Constantine, there are two of you, which is one more than needed."

The count's show of ferocity would have made one of Constantine's coins find a voice. The young man nodded. "I'm Constantine IX, king of Regia. I demand to be treated according to my rank."

"You didn't tell us you were a king," put in Weasel. "Will they pay more for you?"

Las Bombas turned his astonishment on Weasel and Sparrow. "Do you half-size scarecrows have any notion? Do you know what he's worth? A kingdom!"

Theo scarcely heard Las Bombas. He was concerned for Mickle and no one else. She had begun to stir. In a few moments, she opened her eyes. Unlike Luther and Las Bombas, who had hesitated before recognizing Theo, Mickle knew him instantly.

"I said I'd find you." Mickle grinned at him. "What have you done to yourself? You look awful."

The count, beside himself with excitement, broke in to tell Mickle the prisoner's identity.

She finally glanced at Constantine.

"King of Regia? Good. You're just the one I wanted to talk to."

Las Bombas claimed that he had attended a number of princes and dignitaries in his assorted capacities, but he confessed that the cave of the water rats was the most unusual place he had ever seen for a meeting between two monarchs. All the more since it shortly came out, along with Theo's own account, that Queen Mickle had once occupied the same hut as Sparrow and Weasel in The Fingers; and that the pair were on friendliest terms not only with the famous Keller but also with the white-haired old buffer, the queen's own chief minister.

King Constantine, who reluctantly explained his own presence there, accepted her identity as Queen Augusta, further proved by the royal signet she carried.

"The Beggar Queen," he said bitterly. "From now on, I suppose I'll be called the Coward King."

"Connie," put in Sparrow, "I told you not to worry about that."

"I had sent a message to General Erzcour," Constantine went on. "It probably got there the morning you saw him. I told him I was on my way to Eschbach. My uncle agreed I could go. I wanted to see real fighting. I did. If I'd come sooner—"

"You'd have been killed," said Theo, "along with Erzcour."

Constantine bowed his head. "It would have been more honorable than this."

"That's stupid, Connie," said Mickle. "We're both alive. I like it better that way. You saved me a trip to Mull. We can settle things between us right now—if you want to."

"Yes," Constantine said. "I want to end this whole bloody mess. I thought, at first, a nice little war would be marvelous. We all wanted it: Erzcour, Montmollin, my uncle. Cabbarus wanted it most of all. He had a hand in everything from the beginning. I'll deal with him when I get back. For now, I only want it all to stop."

Mickle had begun explaining her plan to the king when Las Bombas put a finger to his lips. "Dear girl," he whispered, "you hold the trump card: a king! His life's at stake. You don't have to give anything. You're a splendid general, but you have much to learn about diplomatic dickering."

Mickle reminded the count that she would have made the offer in any circumstances. Despite his advice, she kept nothing hidden from Constantine. Although he had little choice, he gladly accepted. His spirits had risen. The treaty, he felt, made up for his behavior at Eschbach.

"They won't call me the Coward King now," he said. "I'll be Constantine the Conciliator."

The rest of the meeting went less easily. Mickle, weakened though she was, would have gone immediately with Constantine to Eschbach or the nearest Regian headquarters. Theo was against it. He and Las Bombas agreed that even if the king was dealing in good faith, they had no assurance that Constantine's officers would not close ranks around their monarch and kill his captors out of hand.

The Regian army, furthermore, was already on the march through the Sabrina valley. There was no time to halt it. With or without a treaty, there would be slaughter at La Jolie unless they reached it quickly. The king, Theo insisted, must leave immediately for Florian's camp. He himself would take him. Mickle could follow with Las Bombas and the water rats.

"All right, Connie will go to Florian," said Mickle. "I agree to that, but not to the rest of it. We'll stay together, all of us."

On this point Mickle refused to budge, although Theo protested that she was in no case to travel. He urged her to stay a few days in the care of Las Bombas and the water rats.

"I can ride as well as any of you," said Mickle. "You shot me in the side, not the saddle."

Seeing it was useless trying to make her change her mind, Theo ordered Sparrow and Weasel to pack up their store of provisions and make ready to go. Las Bombas and King Constantine lent them a hand, while Theo stayed a few more moments with Mickle, who had promised to rest until all was prepared.

"Before I started for Mull," she told him, "before I had any notion of what happened to you, my mother said something to me. She said you didn't come back because you'd taken up with someone else."

"She was wrong. You know that."

"Yes," Mickle said, "but sometimes I've wondered since then, even if you hadn't found someone else, how you felt—"

"I sent a message with Luther. I said that I loved you. It seems long ago."

"It was. But it's not long ago anymore. It's now."

"Yes." He hesitated. Mickle was watching him closely. Finally, he said, "Yes, I do love you. Now. As much as I'm able."

Mickle gave him a questioning glance, then said lightly, "Does that mean more? Or less?"

"It only means—" Theo began. "It only means that I've hated so much for so long, I'm sick with it. I don't recognize myself. I'm not even sure I know what loving is."

Mickle nodded. "I suppose," she said quietly, "I'll have to wait until you find out."

# 22

Weasel perched on the saddle with Theo, Sparrow with King Constantine. Discovering that Connie was king of Regia in no way overawed Sparrow. What did impress her was that he had eight ancestors with the same name.

"I don't know how you keep track of them," she told him.

"It isn't easy," said Constantine. "When this is over, you come and visit Breslin Palace. I'll show you pictures of them. There's not much difference, though. We all look rather alike."

"I've already been to a palace," said Sparrow. "It wasn't interesting. Yours might be better. Yes, I'd like to see those ancestors sometime. I don't have any ancestors at all."

"You're lucky. They can be a burden, especially uncles." Constantine said no more. The king of Regia had undergone some new experiences which he had not yet digested. Never before had he been so terrified. Never before had he been punched in the nose. Even so, he had, on his own, made a fine treaty with Augusta. He felt in good spirits and decided that this was not the time to discuss family matters.

Theo did not try to find Justin and his company. They were, surely, following a similar direction. Justin, however, had probably chosen a line of march allowing him to keep to the lower and easier slopes. Theo headed straight through the hills, a path more difficult but shorter. Less encumbered, he hoped to save precious time. With luck, he could reach La Jolie before the week was out.

He pressed on, in all haste, Mickle beside him, Constantine following, and Las Bombas bringing up the rear. Justin, Theo supposed, would demand a court-martial. Of this, he said nothing to Mickle. He was too weary, and too sick at heart, to care about it. He wanted only to bring his party quickly and safely to Florian.

Over the next few days, he made better progress than he had hoped. Mickle kept the pace; but did so, he was aware, with growing difficulty. When he tried to slacken, she insisted on going faster, claiming she was not suffering at all.

It was a pretense even Mickle, with all her skill, could not maintain. Within a few leagues of La Jolie, her wound opened again; she was weaker than ever from loss of blood and exhaustion. Theo had planned to keep on throughout the last night of the march. Instead, he ordered a halt. Mickle, for once, did not protest.

To make matters worse, the king of Regia wrenched his back unsaddling his horse. All the efforts of Las Bombas did nothing to ease Constantine's agony. The king could scarcely move, let alone ride. The water rats were as fresh as when they started, but the count, himself saddlesore and weary, pleaded for a few hours of rest.

So close to Florian's camp, Theo could not bring himself to delay that long. He ordered Las Bombas to tend Mickle and the king while he rode ahead. They were to set out the next day as early as they could. If Mickle and Constantine were unable to travel, Theo would send a party back to help them. He would at least report the news to Florian.

He reached the lowlands a little after dawn. Florian's encampment spread over the meadows of the Montmollin estate, the blackened shell of the great house looming up in the center. He urged the last strength from his mount. Tents had been pitched in the deer park and the gardens, where he glimpsed Jellinek tending a cook fire. Zara came running to him as soon as he jumped down. He saw Musket, armed with saber and pistol. He barely took a moment to embrace the dwarf and the russet divinity; and to catch sight of a young man wearing general's insignia, who had just arrived with the queen's advance guard. Zara motioned Theo to the great house.

In the ruined grand salon, with its shattered casements and shreds of charred drapery blowing like beggars' rags, Florian in his old blue greatcoat sat at a small table with an older man. Between them stood a wine bottle and two glasses. Legs crossed, leaning back at his ease on the remains of a brocaded chair, Florian beckoned to Theo, seeming more preoccupied than astonished.

As quickly as he could, Theo reported what had happened. Instead of rejoicing, Florian took the news calmly and with a bleak smile.

"Strange fortunes of war," he said. "Yesterday, it could have made all the difference in the world. Today, I'm not certain. We've had one engagement already, an expensive one, with the Regian advance columns from the Sabrina valley. Duke Conrad, I understand, is in command. He has even more troops than I expected. General Witz has done his best, but we're far outnumbered. Constantine may be too late to save many lives. We shall, if Conrad has any military sense at all, soon come under a full attack."

Florian broke off. He turned to the older man, who had risen from his chair. "Forgive me. Baron Montmollin, allow me to present one of my officers: Colonel Kestrel, as he pleases to call himself."

Theo started. "Who told you I took that name?"

"There's been much talk of Kestrel," said Florian. "I only guessed. No, more than a guess. An assumption. I know you better than you give me credit for."

Baron Montmollin bowed gracefully. His clothing, stained and a little threadbare, had been carefully brushed. "General Florian and I were discussing a matter of some importance: the quality of this wine. That it was somehow overlooked during a recent visit by my tenants I account a whim of fate. It is the last of a splendid vintage, laid down in the year of my birth.

"The general finds it has a charming bouquet. To my palate, a touch of acidity. Would you care to give your opinion?"

The baron stopped and looked past Theo, who followed his glance. Justin was in the doorway. Theo went to him, hand outstretched. Justin shouldered him aside, and strode up to Florian.

"Your second-in-command has arrived ahead of you," said Florian. "He has interesting news."

"He's not my second-in-command," said Justin. "He has no right to command anything. At Eschbach—"

"I know about that," Florian said. "It has no bearing at the moment. Theo tells me the king of Regia has been captured. If he can be brought here in time, he may be useful. If not—" Florian shrugged. "Meantime, please excuse us. I'll talk with you later. Baron Montmollin and I—"

"Montmollin?" cried Justin. His scar was livid, his face darkened with anger. "You let him live? You sit drinking wine with him? The traitor ought to be shot."

"There will be shooting enough before this day is out," Florian said. "Be patient."

"I say do it now," Justin retorted. "Do it before the Regians attack or they'll snatch him away from us. He must be executed in front of all the troops. We'll have that much justice, no matter what else."

"You would deny me a trial, sir?" put in Montmollin. "I had the impression that a man's right to speak in his own defense was among your noble causes. Or have I misunderstood? Justice, perhaps, may best be served by disregarding it?"

"How dare you even speak the word?" Justin flung back. "Trial? You've been tried and sentenced by every man and woman killed because of your treachery."

"Sir," Montmollin replied, smiling wearily, "I do not recognize the legality of your court."

"Leave us, Justin," Florian said quietly.

Justin did not move. His eye had fallen on a silver-mounted pistol beside the wine bottle. For a moment, Theo expected him to seize the weapon and carry out the sentence then and there.

"Leave us," Florian repeated. "I order you."

Justin turned his furious glance on Florian, who said no more but whose eyes had gone bright and cold. Finally, without another word, Justin spun on his heel and walked out of the room.

Montmollin, silent during this, stood up. "An unsettling interruption, General. Shall we agree that our discussion was inconclusive? Now, if we have no further business—"

Florian rose and bowed to Montmollin. Theo followed Florian from the salon. Only then did Theo give way to his own anger.

"You can't mean to let Montmollin go! No, not shoot him out of hand. Justin was wrong. But the man betrayed the kingdom. You know that. You can't ignore it. He must come to trial."

"He has conducted his own trial," said Florian. "I will not see him in front of a firing squad or on a scaffold. I will not allow it, no matter what he has done. Call it a weakness on my part."

A shot rang from the great house. Florian continued to walk without breaking stride. He did not look back.

"He has rendered a verdict on himself," Florian said. "I want this house burnt to the ground. I want nothing left of it." He halted a moment. "Zara knows. So shall you. No one else. My real name is Montmollin. The baron was my father."

Soon after, Las Bombas galloped into La Jolie with the news: King Constantine was gone.

# 23

"Broke his royal word!" cried Las Bombas. "I'll break his royal neck! Constantine the Conciliator? Conniver, more like it! He never had a thought of keeping his parole. Wrenched his back? I'll give him another kind of lame excuse. I should have known better, I should have tied the little dandy hand and foot."

"If I see him," put in Weasel, shaking his fist, "I'll punch him in the nose again."

Theo had gone to Mickle, helping her dismount. She seemed hardly better than the day before, pale and somewhat feverish from both the pain of her wound and her distress at the king's flight.

"I never thought it of Connie," she murmured. "I really believed we'd come to good terms."

"The only terms left to us," said Florian, "are fight or surrender."

Florian called a last council in his tent. Zara sent for Justin while Theo and General Witz half carried Mickle between them.

"Your Majesty," said Witz, "beg to report that I did all possible. The Regians attacked as I began to withdraw from Altus-Birkenfeld. I was obliged to leave some of the regiments there to hold them back. Here, we are only at half-strength. According to my calculations—"

"Dear Witz," Mickle said to the distraught general, "no one could have done better. None of it matters now. The best of us are here together, whatever happens."

As Theo helped her into Florian's tent, he heard an explosion and a roar like rushing wind. He glanced back. The great house of La Jolie was burning.

Uninvited to the council, Sparrow and Weasel had gone off on their own. That Constantine had broken his word, that most of the army of Westmark stood an excellent chance of being destroyed, that the camp itself could be taken by storm in a matter of hours carried little weight with Sparrow. She had something more urgent in mind.

Keeping a firm grip on Weasel's hand, she strode briskly, unhurried but purposeful and confident, through the horse lines, through the field of tents and the stands of muskets, making her way among the detachments of royal troops and irregulars. She asked for neither directions nor information, navigating as surely as she had ever done on the river.

Only after she had searched most of the encampment did her confidence begin to fray. She had tramped halfway across Westmark, nursed Weasel through his sickness, captured a king, and looked on more death and destruction than she could have imagined. In all this, she had clung only to three certainties: that she, Weasel, and Keller would never come to harm. She had been right, so far, about the first two. The third was now open to question.

Having failed to find the journalist on her own, she decided to inquire among the soldiers. Then she decided not to.

She wanted an answer.

She feared the answer she might get.

At last, near one of the earthworks, Sparrow stopped short. With his back to her, a man was perched on a wooden keg. He was loading a musket. Like his comrades, he wore a red ribbon knotted around the arm of his shabby coat.

"Keller!"

The man turned. His pinched face was the color of dirty clay. He seemed in the grip of some wasting illness. He put down the musket and ramrod.

"Well, I'll be damned—or blessed, as the case may be," said Keller. "It's the water rats."

Sparrow reached him ahead of her brother, and threw her arms around him.

The war, as far as she was concerned, had just ended.

The council could not agree. Witz maintained that they should hold out to the last man, which he counted on being. He sided, however, with Theo, who insisted on sending the queen, with a strong escort, immediately to Marianstat.

Justin, who had spurned Theo's attempt to talk with him about Rina, seemed withdrawn and at odds with everyone else. He spoke only once, declaring that his company, and all the irregulars, should no longer support the queen in a hopeless battle. He was ready to lead his own troops back into the hills, whether Florian agreed or not.

"This is wonderful," Mickle said. "Now we start

bickering among ourselves. That makes it much easier for the Regians. Justin, I'm sorry for what happened, but I won't let you go sulking off like a spoiled child. If it turns out that you're needed here, you'll stay—or you'll have me to deal with. As for Theo, if he expects me to turn and run to save my own neck, he's mistaken. I'll also remind General Witz that we've kept the army together so far and I won't throw it away to no purpose."

"Retreat again?" said Witz. He had counted on proving himself to his monarch by the ultimate sacrifice, and he did not want to be done out of it. "Your Majesty, allow me at least—"

"I'll allow you to follow my orders," Mickle said. "Yes, we'll retreat to the Vespera if we must, and hold a line there."

"With the river at your back," warned Florian. "Even so, I'm not sure you'll have time. My people will cover your retreat, but we may not be able to hold long enough."

"The Regians could outflank us, in any case," put in Zara. "They'll attack you while you're on the march."

"An army retreating is an oyster without a shell," added Las Bombas. "Theo has the right of it. Marianstat's the place for you. I volunteer to make sure you get there— Ah, in fact, I'll go with you."

One of Florian's officers had come in. He went directly to Florian and said something in his ear. Florian smiled bitterly.

"Our choice may be already made for us," he told the others. "It would seem a squadron of cavalry is preparing to engage us. Constantine might have paid us the compliment of sending at least a regiment."

Telling Witz to have all troops stand to their arms, Florian pulled up the collar of his coat and strode from the tent to observe the Regian movements for himself. The others followed, Mickle insisting on going with them.

Theo and Las Bombas held back a few moments. They had foreseen Mickle's refusal to leave for Marianstat. The count had already arranged for Musket to be on hand with Friska and the coach. The dwarf had followed his instructions and was there waiting when Zara and Justin started after Florian.

"Musket knows what to do," Las Bombas murmured to Theo. "If we manage to get her into the coach, he'll set off neck or nothing for Marianstat. Call it kidnapping if you like, but she'll be well out of here." He turned to Mickle. "Get in, dear girl. You'll be more comfortable. We'll ride on, you'll join us."

Mickle, to Theo's relief, gladly accepted to ride in the coach instead of on horseback. The count's vehicle, battered and mud-stained, had been her first headquarters at the Alma. "It might as well be the last," said Mickle, climbing in. "It's the only place now that feels like home."

Theo and the count urged their horses across the stubble fields to the most advanced of the earthworks. Florian was there ahead of them. Hatless, his faded blue greatcoat flapping in the autumn breeze, he stood with a spyglass to his eye. The Regian cavalry had drawn closer, gaining speed.

"If Florian thought a regiment would be a compliment," Las Bombas said dourly, "I don't know what he'd call that, over there. Fulsome flattery?"

The count pointed. Behind the advancing squadron,

the Regian infantry had come into line. To the front and right flank, the troops stretched as far as Theo could see; the sun glinted on the points of their bayonets. He had not dared to say farewell to Mickle; it would have betrayed his plan. He wished now he could have taken a few moments alone with her.

He turned for a last glimpse of the coach. Musket, by now, should have veered off onto the Marianstat road. Theo, alarmed, called out to Las Bombas, who was gloomily watching the Regian lines. The dwarf was driving Friska, with all speed, toward the front.

Theo shouted for Musket to stop. Las Bombas waved furiously at the dwarf.

"Idiot! You've gone the wrong way! Turn around! Go back!"

The dwarf slowed long enough for Mickle to put her head out the window. "I wouldn't be much of a general if I couldn't guess what the enemy might do," she called. "Or, in this case, my friends."

The count shook a fist at the disobedient dwarf. "Do as you're told!"

"I am." Musket grinned and shrugged. "Anything else would be mutiny and insubordination, as I see it. I'm under the queen's orders. She's my commanding officer. She just made me a captain."

Florian was calling to Theo. The Regian cavalry had halted. A handful of officers rode forward. One of them raised a lance from which a banner unfurled, spreading as the breeze plucked it.

"That's no Regian flag," cried Las Bombas. "There's nothing— It's completely white! By heaven, a flag of truce!"

Mickle had heard the count's exclamation; so had

Musket, who halted the coach, uncertain of his orders. Mickle sprang out and climbed to the box beside him. Florian, too, had seen the white flag and had hastily mounted. Before Theo and Las Bombas could do likewise, Mickle snatched the reins, whistled through her teeth, and sent Friska plunging past the earthworks into the open field.

Before Mickle had gone halfway, a slim figure broke from the group of officers and galloped to meet her. Mickle reined up and jumped from the box.

"Connie!"

King Constantine dismounted and ran to her, holding out his hand. "My uncle's back there, and my staff officers. I told them to wait. I want to talk to you first, privately."

"Get out of the wind, then," said Mickle. "You'll catch your death of cold."

Constantine followed her into the coach and began hastily: "Before my uncle and all the rest of them start in—it's going to be formal, official, and all such—between us, you have to know this.

"I once broke my word to Baron Montmollin. I broke it again when I ran away from you and your friends. But it was for a different reason."

Constantine paused a moment, then looked squarely at Mickle. "I'm not all that much of a fool, you know."

"I never took you for one, Connie."

"My uncle doesn't realize it," said Constantine, "but I know very well what he thinks of me as a king. I used to hear him talking to Erzcour. I'm quite aware they both would have been happier if—well, if I were out of the way. He didn't make any effort to stop me when I left for Eschbach. He'd always kept me from going to the front. This time, he didn't seem to mind. I don't mean he planned anything—no, I don't believe he'd have gone so far. Still, he wouldn't have been displeased if I'd met with an accident—as I nearly did."

"Why did you run off?" asked Mickle. "We'd have taken you to Florian's headquarters, you'd have been perfectly safe. We'd have sent word that you were our prisoner, that we were holding you hostage. We'd have had your life in our hands—" Mickle frowned. "Yes, I see what you mean."

"Exactly so," Constantine said ruefully. "As a hostage, I was worth nothing to you. My life in your hands? It would have suited Uncle Conrad very well if you'd killed me. What I'm telling you is a secret, only between monarchs. It's enough that you and I know it, and I'll keep my eye on him in future.

"I went back because Uncle Conrad wouldn't have dared try any tricks, not with all my staff officers around me. And certainly not when I was bringing such a splendid treaty.

"Oh—I hope you have pen and ink," Constantine added. "We'll need them, and state seals, and the whole business, for the official document. I didn't note down any of the terms when we talked about them, but they will be the same, just as you said? I'll take your word for that."

"Yes, Connie," said Mickle, "and I'll take your word, too."

# 24

Torrens was glad of the rain. A fair day would have mocked his mood. He watched from a casement in the ministerial chambers. Despite the weather, all Marianstat had been festive for two days and nights, singing, dancing in the streets, as joyous at the end of the war as they were at its beginning. They had turned out to cheer their queen and her returning troops; they had cheered the parade of city militia; they had cheered Florian and Justin. They believed they were celebrating a victory. Torrens knew better.

Queen Augusta had shown the courage, strength, and intelligence Torrens hoped for in his monarch. She had ended the war honorably. King Constantine, of his own accord, had granted equal concessions, including the rebuilding of towns destroyed by the Regian army and the replenishment of grain lost in the failed harvest. There had been no triumph on either side, though each claimed one. For his part, Torrens had worked miracles. He was not pleased with them.

The queen had held her army together. Torrens had done likewise for the kingdom. He had done more than raise troops, provisions, and arms. He had stiffened the spirit of his people, giving them courage even when his own had failed. From the Juliana Palace, he had announced victories in battles that had never been fought, in places that were only names on a map. He had proclaimed stern laws against those who spoke or wrote or published questioning the conduct of the war, and sternly carried them out. He applied justice, recognizing it was injustice. Had he done less, he knew beyond a doubt that, for all her efforts, Augusta would have lost. He had convinced her subjects of certain victory. And so, as far as they were concerned, Westmark had defeated Regia. Torrens had only defeated himself.

Queen Caroline sat on a couch near his desk. If Torrens had given his strength to the kingdom, Caroline had given hers to him. Torrens found this ironic. In the days of Cabbarus, he had been the one who supported her. Now it had turned to the contrary. Caroline continued to astonish him. He was deeply troubled over Florian and Justin, but Caroline received them both at the palace. Today, she had come to inquire if her daughter had taken up the question of medals and decorations, and to learn the chief minister's attitude.

Torrens turned away from the casement. "Queen Augusta has not yet discussed the matter with me. I am not sure what the government's policy should be. That they deserve highest honor for bravery I freely admit. The queen must also be aware that Florian and Justin have gained widespread support for their cause. However, their cause is not ours. To decorate them would appear to give official approval, to encourage them in their future actions."

"They should be given the Star of Westmark for what

they have done," said Caroline, "not what they may do. They conducted themselves with utmost gallantry, with the selfless devotion of true heroes, as did all our brave soliders—"

Caroline broke off. Her daughter had come into the chamber. "My dear child, Dr. Torrens and I have been discussing—"

"Yes," Mickle said, "I heard."

Torrens went to her. She drew away from him, and from her mother's outstretched arms. "Do either of you believe a word of what you've been saying? Yes, I think you really do, and that's the worst of it."

Caroline frowned. "Do you not approve? You, more than anyone, must know how well deserved—"

"I approve," said Mickle. "Yes, by all means. For gallantry? If you want to call it that. For turning themselves into beasts for the sake of the kingdom? Yes, give them a piece of gold and a ribbon. Give medals to the dead, while you're at it."

Caroline turned to Torrens. "What has put my daughter in such a state? Please, Doctor, see to her. I will send for Theo."

"Theo?" cried Mickle. "Yes, send for him. Send for him if you can. Do you know where he is? I don't. He's gone."

Theo had vanished: not from Marianstat, but from himself. What he least wanted to remember he had not been allowed to forget. He did not know how it had happened, but word had spread through the city. The Marianstatters were overjoyed. The gallant Colonel Kestrel was none other than their own future prince consort. His private shame had become a matter of public pride.

He had not turned for help to Las Bombas, his friend. He had not turned to Florian, whom he admired. He had not turned to Mickle, whom he loved; least of all to her. He had, first, gone into the city to make certain purchases. What he could not buy in the shops, he gathered from the pavements and gutters. Hatless, cloakless, sopping wet, he found his way to Keller's offices. He could think of no better place to hide.

He asked Keller for two things: secrecy and a spare room. The journalist, whose health had been noticeably damaged, was delighted to grant him both.

"I went through the war without a scratch," said Keller. "All I acquired in line of duty was a chest cold. It seems to have become a permanent companion. I'm much too ill to trust myself to a doctor's hands, and not ill enough to consult an undertaker. Sparrow and Madam Bertha do quite well for me. They'll see to anything you need."

"I don't need anything," said Theo, which was not true. He had survived the war; he was not sure he could survive the peace. He hoped, as a last resort, he could unburden his heart by unburdening his memory.

He stayed, for the next few days, in Keller's garret. The journalist had given strict orders that his guest was not to be disturbed. The orders were partially obeyed, which was more than Keller had come to expect since his own return. He had forbidden his water rats to fuss over himself: an instruction they entirely disregarded. With Theo, they behaved a little better.

Sparrow and Weasel always found some excuse to

loiter around Theo's closed door. Weasel accidentally found himself in a position with his eye to the keyhole. Sparrow smacked him in the ear for it. She had become acutely conscious of proper manners. Spying at keyholes she found discourteous and rude. Instead, she peered through the crack under the door. She only gained dust in her eye.

"Serves you right," said Weasel, rubbing his smarting ear.

Madam Bertha intruded in her own fashion. She insisted on leaving trays of food; then, insulted because her cooking had gone untasted, grumbled at Keller.

The journalist was the only one who respected Theo's privacy. Yet, after a time even Keller wondered, concerned, about his houseguest. Excusing himself on the grounds of journalistic license, which he felt permitted him to nose wherever it suited him, he went upstairs one morning.

The door was open. Theo was sitting on a stool. Sheets of paper covered the table and littered the floor in front of him. Without specific invitation, Keller stepped inside. Theo glanced around at him. Keller saw that his eyes were bloodshot, his face hollow, but without the haunted air it had when he first came. He looked as if an abscess in his mind had broken and drained.

"So that's what you've been up to." Keller bent over the papers, astonished not only at the number of wash drawings but, as much, at the subjects. There were many portraits: some of Theo himself; more of Mickle, Florian, Justin, and others Keller did not recognize.

"A man we used to call the Monkey," said Theo, pointing at one. "This—a boy who died in Justin's tent,

I don't know his name. The others—they'd mean nothing to anyone else. I remember them."

Keller examined each one. In addition to the portraits, and in greater quantity, were sketches of scenes: a torn body he could only guess was the poet, Stock; an uprising in the streets of a town; a shape dangling from a shattered window.

Keller, overcoming his first surprise, forgot that Theo would one day be his sovereign and studied the work with detached professional judgment.

"All in all, quite good. No, I should say better than that," observed the journalist. "Yes, excellent. Untrained, but excellent despite that. Perhaps, indeed, because of that. I find them unsettling, which is what they should be. How often I'd want to look at them—well, they're hardly decorative. They take getting used to."

"Yes," said Theo. "They would take getting used to."

"What will you do with them?"

"I don't know. Nothing."

"In that case," said Keller, "allow me to keep them."

"As you please."

"What strikes me," the journalist went on, "is something curious. You've done these with ink and water, but your ink puzzles me. It gives quite a remarkable effect. It would almost seem that you mixed grit, or mud—"

"From the street," said Theo. "From sweepings, from gutters. Perhaps I should have used blood, but too much has been used."

"Permit me to offer you even higher compliments," said Keller. "You've managed to turn dust into art. So many of us do the opposite."

# 25

He had, finally, gone back to the Juliana. Mickle did not question his absence. Theo wondered if Keller, despite his promise, had taken it on himself to tell her where he was. He had no time to look into that. Mickle had called for a council, to be held not in the grand hall of state but in one of the smaller chambers.

They had waited for him. Las Bombas was in his most spectacular uniform. Florian and Justin, in common clothing, had kept their red armbands. Mickle had dressed as the commanding officer of her Old Guard. Beside her, General Witz had prepared stacks of paper for his notes and calculations. Torrens was there with Queen Caroline, although Theo did not learn until later that Justin had angrily objected to their presence.

"General Florian and I have already talked about a constitution," Mickle announced when all had settled themselves around the table. "Since he has a number of provisions in mind, I've asked him to make a draft and present it to us later. The question we haven't settled is the place of the monarch in our new government."

Justin began to speak. Mickle raised a hand and continued. "Or—if there's any place at all for one. As far as I'm concerned, I'll tell you this: When it turned out that I was Princess Augusta—Queen Augusta, sooner or later—I hoped there'd be some relative or other who'd like the throne better than I did. But I couldn't find one. I don't want the throne now any more than I did then. So, I'd like to start with the matter of my abdication."

"That is not possible," Queen Caroline broke in. "You were born to be queen of Westmark. So you are, and shall be."

"Madam, on the contrary," said Florian. "She was not born to be queen of Westmark, but to be a human, like us all. The privileges of birth come quite by accident."

"You misunderstand me, sir," Caroline replied. "I speak of royalty, not aristocracy. Dr. Torrens and I have talked of this at length, these past months, and I have come to agree with him. There is no reason why the child of an aristocrat should, by accident, as you say, enjoy rights denied the child of a commoner.

"But royalty is not only a matter of birth but also of special grace. The late king, my husband, was a good man; a weak king perhaps, but a king nonetheless, with his own portion of that grace. It is laid upon the monarch—no, it is set within the monarch. It can be neither escaped nor renounced. It cannot be abdicated."

"I can't say one way or the other about that," returned Mickle. "All I wanted to tell you is that I've considered letting someone else head the government. If you want the hard truth, I don't trust anyone here not to botch it up—with all the best intentions. Not even Florian. Certainly not you, Justin. So, as for giving up the throne, I've decided: I won't."

Justin reddened angrily. "You may not have the choice. My people are still under arms. We can force you to abdicate."

"Can you?" Mickle looked straight at him. "Do you want to try?"

"Majesty," put in Witz, scribbling on his papers, "beg to report: According to my calculations, it would be most inadvisable for Colonel Justin to attempt it. Inadvisable for General Florian, as well."

"I don't intend to," said Florian. "Not at the moment. What may come about someday doesn't concern me now. The existence of a monarch is less important than forming a government. Temporary it may be, but we must have one."

"You shall form it without me," said Torrens, who had been listening silently to this exchange. "I ask Queen Augusta to dismiss me. If she will not, then I hereby resign my office."

"You have served two monarchs," Caroline said softly to Torrens. "You have served them well as councillor." She laid her hand on his. "Will you now serve me as my dear friend?"

Torrens bowed his head. "Yes, as I have always wished to do."

"I would consent to a monarch," Florian went on, "but only if the monarch is limited, and bound by the same constitution that binds all of us."

"Let her keep her throne, then. It's meaningless," said Justin. "The chief minister will hold the real power. That must be one of us, Florian. You or me."

"Not necessarily." Florian turned to Theo. "Do you remember when we talked about old Jacobus? You were a great believer in his idea of three consuls. I didn't agree with you at the time, but I've come to think we should try it. Three sharing power would be less dangerous than power in a single pair of hands."

"That depends," Justin put in sharply. "Whom do you propose?"

"Myself, for one," said Florian. "You, for another."

"And whom else?"

"For a third, I name Theo."

Before Theo could reply, Justin sprang to his feet. "No! I won't have him as one of us."

"He's the best choice," Florian said. "If you still bear him any ill will, I advise you to put it aside."

"That has nothing to do with it," Justin flung back. "If I agree to three consuls, I insist they must all be commoners."

Florian nodded. "Yes, they must be. And so he is."

"He's not!" cried Justin. "He'll be prince consort. That makes him part and parcel of the monarchy. His interest will be theirs, not ours. My people won't stand for it. Neither will yours."

"He's not prince consort yet," replied Florian, "nor will be until he and Augusta marry."

"Which occasion I am in process of arranging," said Las Bombas. "For the ceremony, I have absolutely dazzling plans."

"I'm sure you do," said Florian. "You'll have to put them off."

"He will not," declared Theo. "Mickle and I have waited long enough. We have a right to our own happiness."

"You also have a debt," said Florian. "I remind you of that day at Kopple's mill."

"I promised I'd support your cause. I've done it. I've fought in the war—"

"That was your choice, not mine," Florian said. "As I see it, the debt remains. If you wish to repay it, you'll serve with us. I'll count that as truly keeping your word.

"It's up to you. I can't force you," Florian continued. "At the mill, I gave you a first lesson in statecraft. I might have given you a second: Statesmen often find it convenient to forget their promises."

"Hold on a minute," put in Mickle. "I have a say in this, too. Theo's right. We've waited far too long. I want Las Bombas to go ahead with his plans. I want to marry without another moment's delay."

Then she added to Theo, "That's me speaking as me. Speaking as queen, as Torrens taught me, I want you to join Florian and Justin."

"But—why?" Theo burst out, dismayed. "I'd be no help. They're already at odds. The war hasn't ended, it's just begun: in the council chamber."

"I'd rather have it there than on a battlefield," said Mickle. "I'll count on you to settle their differences reasonably. And, after all, you did give Florian your word."

Theo was silent for a long moment. He smiled ruefully at Mickle. "Yes. I'll keep it. I'll serve with them. But I'm not a statesman."

"I know," said Mickle. "That's one of your better qualities."